The Small Tortoiseshell

Derek Francis Allen

For Chris, Beccy and Michael
with the promise that this really is a work of fiction.

PREFACE

This book began life as an Open University assignment in the field of Arts and Humanities. The aim was to write the beginning of a story from a given sentence and from this came the idea of the train and the name 'Kay'. I completed the assignment as far as it went and got a good mark for it but I couldn't leave the characters, Kay and Em, respectively in an old Ford Escort and a small terraced house in Watford. I just had to know what adventures my brain had in store for them. And so *The Small Tortoiseshell* was born.

Chapter One

Tuesday April 14th 2009

Every new beginning itself has to have a beginning and for Kay it came on the 18.15 heading north from Baker Street. He had a good memory but even so his recall of the events of that day was astonishing. He remembered his breakfast toast being slightly burnt, dropping into The Globe for a quick pint at lunchtime with half a dozen colleagues - he could name them if he tried, and even the phone call he had received from a disgruntled customer in Worthing at a quarter past three. But as he sat on the train reading *The Evening Standard*, Kay was at that moment entirely unaware that Tuesday April 14th 2009 was destined to become lodged in his hippocampus and would, in all probability remain there for the rest of his life.

*

The elderly Metropolitan Line train slowly ground its way through the north western suburbs of London. Wembley Park. Preston Road. Northwick Park... By the time it had reached Harrow-on-the-Hill, Kay had become more aware of the girl sitting next to him. He usually remained awake on his journey from Moorgate to Chorleywood and was used to a stream of young women getting on the train at any one of the stations out of the city. It was therefore not at all surprising that the pretty girl that got on at Baker Street received a brief glance from Kay and no more. But at some point on that amorphous stretch of line around West Hampstead and Dollis Hill she had settled in her seat and was now fast asleep with her head inclining towards him. 'A liquid lunch in one of the West End's scores of wine bars', he thought. He shifted his position to look at her more closely. She was quite short, no more than one metre fifty five he estimated, with long dark hair and a coffee-coloured complexion that hinted at an interestingly mixed heritage. Her clothing was standard fare for the time, blue jeans, a Hard Rock Café tee-shirt and well-worn Nike trainers. But what really took his eye was that, asleep as she was, her face had taken on a Mona Lisa-like quality with just the hint of a smile on her lips. Some otherwise very pleasant people look frightful when they are asleep. This girl was not one of them.

A rough journey was the lot of those unfortunate enough to have been travelling in the Metropolitan Line's old 'A' stock in the late noughties, especially over the bogies where Kay and the girl were seated. As the train approached Rickmansworth it hit an especially badly maintained section of track and the luckless travellers were violently bounced in their seats. She woke up immediately and through bleary eyes peered out of the almost opaque window.

'Shit', she said in a voice that caused the commuter opposite to raise his eyes from that morning's *Daily Telegraph* crossword and stare at her fiercely.

There is an unwritten charter subscribed to by millions of commuters which states quite clearly that one should never, ever speak to a stranger on a train. Kay broke the rule.

'Are you okay?' he said gently.

'I meant to change at the last station. Shit, shit, shit, shit, shit' she repeated with the emphasis on the last 'shit'.

Kay sympathised, 'Don't worry, you can easily cross platforms. There are plenty of trains this time of day. It won't delay you too much'.

The train pulled into the station and slowed to a halt. There was a brief pause and the sliding doors opened just as an announcement came over the Tannoy, '*London Underground regrets to inform you that due to a signalling failure in the Moor Park area, all southbound services are currently suspended*'. The girl turned to Kay with something approaching panic in her eyes.

'Look, my car's near the next station', he smiled, 'I'll happily give you a lift'.

Silently she looked at Kay, then at the station sign that said 'Rickmansworth' in bold letters. Reluctantly she got off the train but just as the doors had started to close she jumped back on again.

'Would you mind?', she said. 'I'd be really grateful'. She looked at him with a smile, the warmth of which lifted his heart.

Kay was not naïve enough to think other than that this was a big risk for the girl to take. He could have been a rapist, a murderer, perhaps both. But he also realised that the serendipitous way events had unfolded tended to make that possibility very unlikely. Clearly from her point of view it was a risk worth taking.

'I'm so sorry to put you to such trouble', she said, 'it's my niece's birthday today and I promised my sister I'd get there before she went to bed'.

For the first time Kay noticed that she was carrying a plastic Tesco bag, presumably a present or presents for a small child.

'Where does your sister live?' asked Kay.

'Watford' the girl replied. Kay's heart sank. To him, Watford was an urban sprawl. He knew how to get to it and indeed through it but the complexities of the town's internal workings eluded him. Sensing his concern she said cheerfully, 'Don't worry I'll show you the way'. She smiled again and his spirits responded.

The remainder of the short journey between Rickmansworth and Chorleywood was passed in silence. Not that awkward silence that usually passes between strangers but an easy, comfortable silence as if they had been friends all their lives.

This gave Kay the opportunity to study the girl, now sitting opposite him, in greater detail. Quite simply she was stunning. Not pretty-pretty, but stunning in a healthy athletic kind of way. She was not fat but she certainly was not thin. Despite her lack of stature she could easily have been a sportswoman or perhaps a dancer...

*

Kay's car was nothing to write home about, a bog-standard Escort, nine years old and like a faithful old Labrador, beginning to show its age. He tended to keep it clean and tidy though so he was not too embarrassed when he opened the door and let her in.

They had not been driving for long when he said, 'I hope you wouldn't mind if I asked you your name?'

'Of course not, it's Em' she replied.

'Short for Emma?' he ventured.

She lowered her voice and sheepishly whispered, 'Maude.'

Kay's first impulse was to laugh but suppressing this feeling, he considered for a moment. His name was the result of considerable reduction itself, being the ultimate shortening of Kenneth. He had no idea why his parents had called him Kenneth, a name which had seen brief popularity in the early years of the 20th century, gradually tailing off through the 1950s and 60s until they didn't call kids Kenneth anymore, he was the last of a dying breed. But this gave them something in common. They both had ridiculous old-fashioned names that had been reduced to a single letter!

'Hi Em, I'm Kay' he said with what he hoped was a hint of humour in his voice. A further thought immediately came to him; if they had nothing else between them, they did at least have the postcode for Milton Keynes. Again he suppressed a laugh. It would take too long to explain.

Kay hated those awful parties where unspeakably boring people approach you with the words, '*and what do you do*?' but this girl intrigued him and he struggled to stop himself from broaching the subject. There was something about her that said she wasn't a medic, an articled clerk or even worse, a trainee accountant. Fortunately for him, she breached the silence first.

'I'm guessing from your dress that you're something in the city'.

Kay laughed, 'and how on Earth did you deduce that?'.

'It might be something to do with that thing from Tie Rack round your neck and the regulation pin-striped suit', she said, and then with a hint of concern in her voice, 'You don't like it much, do you?'

Kay was crestfallen. On the merest of acquaintances she had seen right through him. 'I hate it' he said with years of pent up feeling.

'Then why do you do it?'.

She had him on the ropes now and he could think of nothing better to say than, 'It pays the bills'.

Following her directions they were now in an older part of town typified by small red brick terraced houses.

'Take the next right and it's the fourth house on the left' she said.

There was a space outside the house and he stopped there.

'I'm so, so grateful' she said, 'you're my hero.' And with that she leaned over and kissed him on the cheek.

Kay was so taken aback that he was unable to speak for a crucial few seconds. She opened the door, turned to him, smiled and said, 'Follow your dreams'.

Closing the door, she blew him a kiss and was gone.

Chapter Two

Spring 2009 - Spring 2010

'Look' said Mike Hancock, 'there's no doubt that you're good at what you do...'

'Thanks for that' said Kay trying not to sound too sarcastic.

'... but I always get the impression you're holding something back. You're content to be a squad player when you could be a star striker'.

This was unusual, a home-spun analogy. Mike was fond of excruciating clichés which had the ability to make his colleagues cringe with embarrassment. Meetings with Mike were like being assaulted by a dictionary of business jargon. His conversation was littered with paradigm shifts, low-hanging fruit, rain-checks, back burners, blue sky thinking, moving the goalposts and key takeaways. Some of the more junior staff at Gresham & Bailey had taken to running a book on which particular expression he would come out with next.

Fundamentally however, Mike was a decent enough guy but he lacked imagination and original thought. He was also in many people's eyes living proof of the 'level of incompetence' theory. The cache of vintage pornography that he kept in his bottom left hand drawer however, made him popular among the Friday afternoon drinking set…

Mike's boss, Tony Bailey (there was no 'Gresham', that was just a name that had the right 'City' feel about it), was driven, stubborn and difficult to work with. With his favoured customers he simply oozed charm and bonhomie but his employees saw a different side of Tony. A previous colleague of Kay's had described him as a one-man slime factory and there was no question that with the aid of outrageous flattery and expensive business lunches he excelled at doing business with whoever made the decision on insurance in small and medium sized companies. Without the incentive of an imminent sale however, he could be a bully to his employees and when it came to accepting responsibility for his errors, he was as slippery as an eel. In this, he was no different to many city bosses but it certainly did not endear him to his staff.

Mike finished his meeting with Kay with a 'more bang for the company's buck' and 'giving 110%' to which Kay replied with a 'game changer' and two 'paradigm shifts'. Mike never seemed to notice his colleagues' mimicry which made it all the more fun to see how many examples of gobbledygook they could get away with. Jayne Bentley from the Motor section claimed to have sneaked seven 'blue sky thinkings' into one sixty second conversation and still Mike hadn't twigged.

Kay returned to his desk and after a moment or two his mind drifted to the events of the previous evening. There was no doubt that he was drawn to the girl, not only for her beauty but for her perception and speed of thought, an ability that he now wished he had possessed or she would not have left without surrendering her phone number. To make matters worse he had already forgotten where in the maze of Watford back streets, her sister had lived. Still, he hung onto the hope that their paths would cross again one day but there seemed little chance of that happening.

*

Three weeks later, in a manner of speaking, their paths did cross. Eastenders was not Kay's cup of tea. In fact he had seldom seen more than a few minutes of the programme since the days of Dirty Den when the viewing habits of Paula, his elder sister, had left him little choice but to absorb enough of the London Borough of Walford to last a lifetime. So, flicking through the channels it was certainly not his intention to stay more than a second or two in the Queen Vic.

Pointing the remote at the TV he was poised to see what was on Channel 4 when something, or more correctly someone, caused him to stop and stare at the screen. There, sitting at a table and drinking what looked like white wine but was probably just slightly tinted water, was Em!

The scene only lasted for a few seconds but it caused him to abandon his move to Channel 4 and watch the rest of the programme. She did not appear again and hardly surprisingly her name was absent from the credits at the end.

*

Spring turned into Summer and Summer into Autumn but still Kay's meeting with the beautiful Em refused to leave his mind. Then at the end of October, another reminder, this time in the form of an advert for shampoo. Kay's heart started racing. Em had been filmed wrapped in a towel, sensually washing her hair. And the advert was repeated time and time again. All through the Autumn and the ensuing Winter the campaign continued, never letting Kay forget the opportunity he had missed.

Of course he didn't know her personal circumstances. She could have been co-habiting with an Olympic weightlifter for all he was aware, someone who could pick him up by the scruff of the neck and kick him through a plate glass window. Thinking about it, other than having a sister that lived in Watford, all he knew was that her name was Maude but she called herself Em. Briefly he wondered how many people knew her real first name. The thought pleased him. Few casual acquaintances knew that he was really Kenneth (or Kenny as his mother still insisted on calling him) and he suspected that it was the same with Em.

Kay was becoming obsessed. He knew that. But with the constant reminders on TV, it was impossible to get her out of his system.

It occurred to him that being in the acting profession it really ought not to be too difficult to track her down. Actors aren't shrinking violets after all, they have agents and agents are usually quite keen to bring their clients to the attention of as many people as possible. But the truth of it was, he didn't know where to start.

It didn't take him long though to realise that acting agencies would be using the internet to post pictures of their clients.

But… there would potentially be thousands of actors in London, every single one would have an agent so all he had to do was find Em amongst the myriad of smiling faces on his computer screen!

He made a start the following day during his lunch break. There were plenty of agents but he wasn't sure how many of them actually published photographs of their clients without some idea of who was likely to be looking. On the first day he drew a blank despite continuing the search at home in the evening. It was clear that many of them required an email before they would send details of their clients and for obvious reasons this was something he could not do even if it were feasible. It was clear that he was barking up the wrong tree.

So he tried a different approach. He googled *'How do you find the name of an actor in a TV commercial?'* This provided a range of responses, mostly directing him to various websites, none of which proved that helpful. Finally, he tried the direct approach; *'Who is the actress in the Sunray Shampoo advert?'*. It surprised him somewhat (or perhaps not he thought on reflection) that he wasn't the only person to ask the question. Google directed him to a rather anonymous message board where 'Mac74' had already broached the subject although he had spelt 'shampoo' as 'shampo'. Sadly though, no-one had replied. Kay noticed however that the message had been posted less than twenty four hours before, so perhaps that was to be expected. He bookmarked the page and packed it in for the day.

The following morning he checked the message board. Nothing. And the day after that, and the day after that… After ten days he was beginning to think that this was a non-starter, so in desperation, he tried yet another tactic. He got in his car and drove round and round Watford just trying to remember where her sister lived. This was a forlorn hope because he really wasn't sure what he was going to do if he ever found the place. But in the event he got himself hopelessly lost and found nothing, just a confusion of little streets, each seemingly identical to its neighbour.

Next day, success! Somebody calling themselves 'Tina' had left the simple message, *'Her name is Emma Silvester'* and that was it. No explanation of how they knew but assuming she had expanded Em to Emma it seemed reasonable.

Ignoring his work he immediately googled 'Emma Silvester'. He found a few plays, television programmes and theatrical productions in which she had played minor parts but on the whole the internet is better at telling you what has happened rather than what is currently happening, or is about to happen. So, he found himself first of all accessing *Time Out* and then checking each play individually. This was not only laborious but was always going to be a long shot. He didn't hold out much hope of success and after an hour or more of searching, he'd got nowhere. Then, *Bingo!* He found her playing the part of *Helene* in a production of *'A Doll's House'* at the National Theatre. Somehow he hadn't seen period drama, especially something as cerebral as Ibsen, as being quite her thing.

The play was only on for a short run and was due to end that Saturday. If he was to have any chance of meeting her, it seemed unlikely that going on the last night would be particularly productive, there would probably be a last night party, fond farewells, that sort of thing. So, entirely at random, he settled on the Wednesday.

In his mind he was troubled by the thought of his appearing to be stalking her. But what constituted stalking? All he was doing was trying to meet a woman to whom he was attracted. What was wrong with that? It was what made the world go round. He knew that his father had relentlessly pursued the pretty half-Jewish girl who would later become his mother and nobody had thought of it as anything other than normal courtship behaviour. If he met Em again and she told him to piss off, that would be an end to it he told himself, he would go away a sadder but wiser man.

Nevertheless, he thought it sensible to let someone else in on the secret so he asked Raj Banerjee, a friend from the office if he fancied going to a play at the National. Raj was hesitant at first,

'Ibsen? Sounds like a cure for insomnia', he said.

'Look I met one of the actresses on the train a little while ago', replied Kay with a knowing smile.

'And you want to get into her knickers' interjected Raj, which, if coarse, contained rather more than a grain of truth. 'Okay, why not?' Raj continued 'I'm not doing anything that evening'.

So Kay bought two tickets as close to the stage as he could for the Wednesday, two days hence. In the meantime he would try to keep his heartbeat from going off the scale.

Chapter Three

Kay had been born into a comfortable middle-class home in Amersham. His father was an accountant and his mother an economics teacher at a local grammar school. Their summer holidays were invariably spent abroad, usually in Spain, France or Italy and one memorable year they had holidayed in Florida including a visit to Walt Disney World which enthralled the eight year old Kay.

He was brought up in a family with no '-isms'. His parents' occupations were of roughly equal standing and he was taught that colour really was only skin deep. This was why, some twenty years later when he met a pretty mixed-race girl on a train, he thought her skin tone 'attractive' and didn't even consider any historical or cultural reasons for her colour let alone how it might obstruct any relationship he wished to have with her. A generation earlier, a relationship would have been tricky, two generations, very difficult and three virtually impossible.

Kay had been a bright pupil and passed the Twelve Plus exam, then current in his home county, with ease. Carefully avoiding the school where his mother taught, he spent his teenage years at another Grammar School three miles away.

From an early age it became clear that he had a talent for sport in general and football in particular. Although neither he nor his father knew it, football ran in his genes. His great great grandfather had played for Everton in the inaugural Football League season of 1888-9 and for some seasons after. And the connection didn't end there, his ancestor had been what was then known as a right half which, allowing for some change in the terminology was exactly Kay's position. Both were fast, hard tackling players with a more than useful shot. The word soon got out and in no time anonymous men in blue anoraks could be seen on the touchlines of his school matches. After considering several offers with his parents, at the age of thirteen he (or more correctly his father) signed a schoolboy contract with Queen's Park Rangers. Shortly after his fifteenth birthday he made his debut in the FA Youth Cup and scored his first goal in the second round at home to Crystal Palace. The following year the club offered him a scholarship contract which he eagerly accepted.

All appeared to be going swimmingly for Kay until an away fixture in the West Midlands during which he came up against a cross between a giraffe and a grizzly bear in the form of Walsall central defender Wayne Selby. In one brief and agonizing moment his left leg was broken in two places. He would eventually recover to play local league football but any ambitions of playing professionally in the Football League were dashed.

Such disappointment is difficult to take at any age but at sixteen it was devastating. The career he had mapped out before him was gone and suspended on a pair of crutches he had to return to school to study for his A levels.

He had always shown an interest in nature and during this dark time he sought solace in the creatures that visited his parents' garden. He soon learnt to recognise all the birds that were likely to visit as well as their calls. Butterflies fascinated him with their bright colours and he even got to know the several species of bumble bee that foraged for nectar amongst the flowers.

He loved all the visitors to the garden but would admit to a particular soft spot for the long-tailed tits. He loved the way they arrived once a day, methodically investigated the garden for grubs and insects, twittered among themselves for a bit and then moved on, as sure as clockwork returning the next day. Their only rival for his affections was a solitary hedgehog, whom he called Sid, who would root around near the compost heap in the evenings.

Although the physical injuries would inevitably take time to heal, his diminutive friends paid no small part in mending the mental hurt he had suffered.

His A levels went far better than he expected and armed with two As and a B he obtained a place at Sussex University. Following much persuasion by his mother, he had opted to read economics. This he soon realised was a mistake - he found the subject dull and remote from the lives of the vast bulk of humanity. Nonetheless he persevered in as much as his active social life would let him.

University was a heaving morass of hormones with thousands of undergraduates trying their hardest to get laid. With his sporting physique and the hard luck story concerning the footballing career that was nearly his, Kay was in prime position to take advantage. A long procession of young women emerged from his room in the mornings, or he emerged from theirs. It was all the same to him.

Then, towards the end of his second year he met Vicky.

Vicky was tall, blonde, captain of the university basketball team and she and Kay found they had much in common. The procession of young women stopped and only Vicky would be seen of a morning, looking distinctly pleased with herself.

Eventually Kay's university days came to an end. Despite his distaste for economics he achieved a 2:1 and proceeded to look for a career which might suit his qualifications. He found the job specifications daunting. Most adverts seemed to want a super-hero not a twenty one year-old graduate with little experience of the world and uncertain self-confidence. Nonetheless, he was eventually offered a position by a large insurance company with an office in Bishopsgate. Two changes of employer later he found himself working for Gresham & Bailey.

Vicky in the meantime had used her law degree to land a job with Clapham based solicitors Hepplewhite, Riches & Partners and had started on the long road towards qualifying as a solicitor herself.

The two of them had moved into a small second-floor flat in Balham with dry rot, a leaking tap and neighbours who belonged to some bizarre fundamentalist religion that seemed to require them to be chanting at random times during both day and night.

For a while they were happy, but Vicky's constant studying tended to restrict their social life and evenings-in watching television became the norm for Kay. Although many of their friends and certainly their parents expected them to announce their impending marriage at any time, somehow it wasn't working. There were no blazing rows, no throwing of crockery, just a general underlying feeling that they weren't getting the best out of each other.

Their break-up was entirely amicable as befitted two people with a genteel upbringing. There weren't even any serious disagreements over the collection of CDs they had amassed during their time together. Some years later when Vicky was marrying another solicitor from her practice she even sent Kay an invite to the wedding, although he considered it wise to politely decline. He was genuinely happy for her though.

With some sadness he moved out of their flat and took a lease on an apartment in Chorleywood, not far from his parents' home. Although most had left the area, he still had some friends there who would help him to get his life back on track or at the very least provide drinking companions for a Friday night.

Chapter Four

Kay was on a knife edge all day. He got through very little work and during an internal meeting he just couldn't concentrate which resulted in Mike making a comment suggesting that Kay was 'not on his game' today.

Tony was more explicit, 'Kay, are you fucking listening?'

'Sorry Tony, I'm not a hundred percent today' replied Kay defensively.

The day dragged on and Kay grew tired of looking at his watch – five past, ten past, quarter past… By five thirty he had had enough. Not wishing to trust the tube, he collected Raj and the two of them walked down Bishopsgate, across London Wall, down Threadneedle Street past Bank Station, eventually ending up on the Embankment and from there across Waterloo Bridge.

They were of course far too early, so they bought coffee at one of the small cafés along the South Bank and slowly drank it while strolling along avoiding hurrying commuters and kids on skateboards in seemingly equal measure.

'I hope this girl you seem besotted with is worth it' said Raj, not entirely relishing the evening but going along to keep his friend company.

With half an hour to go, they entered the Lyttleton Theatre and went to their seats. Kay had taken the opportunity to buy a programme and he thumbed through it to see if it said anything about Em. Under a small stock picture (which was definitely her) he learnt that she was born in West London and had attended RADA from 2006 to 2009. That was all there was, but it had increased his knowledge by a thousand percent. When the curtain went up the theatre was only two-thirds full; the seats around them being largely empty which meant that they stood out a bit, but so what…

When Em entered the stage, he took a sharp intake of breath. She was dressed as a Victorian maid and he could just make out her shape below the costume. The play was frankly passing him by but then being entertained by the performance was not his prime purpose. Nonetheless, it would be handy to pick up a little of the plot, just in case… Once or twice he thought she'd spotted him in the audience but he couldn't be sure and bearing in mind she had only met him once, that seemed frankly unlikely.

One thing he noticed though was that she could act. Boy, could she act. Far better than any of the bigger names above her in the programme he thought, but then he was biased. At the interval he and Raj went to the bar.

'Well what do you think?' asked Kay.

'The play was written for cleverer people than me' replied Raj 'but the girl's a real babe'.

'Isn't she!' said Kay

When the curtain went up again, he tried to concentrate on the play but every time Em was on stage, he lost track.

At the curtain call, Kay clapped enthusiastically although he had no more idea of the plot then than he had when he entered the theatre at 7 o'clock. He and Raj adjourned to a pub not far from the theatre where they remained until just after eleven.

'I think I'd better slope off now' said Raj.

'Okay but I think I'll hang around a bit longer' replied Kay.

Raj rolled his eyes, 'What makes you think an actress you met briefly on a train last year is going to remember you? She's probably shagging some millionaire film director by now'.

'Hope springs eternal in the human breast,' replied Kay, 'Anyway, I thought we clicked last time so it's worth a try…'.

Raj shook his head sadly and blew out his cheeks, 'well, best of luck. If I were a bookmaker I'd give you a hundred to one against'.

And with that he headed off towards Waterloo Station. Kay hung around for a bit longer, then slowly retraced his steps to the theatre hoping that he would bump into Em en route to the station. It was a long shot, he knew that and if he stayed much beyond midnight he would be in danger of missing his last train home. He was just about to call it a day when, against all the odds, there she was!

But she wasn't alone. A tall man in denims whom Kay didn't recognise as one of the cast members was walking along with her. 'Shit' thought Kay putting the worst possible interpretation on the situation. Em and the tall man walked slowly towards the station and when they got there they both made for the underground platforms. Kay followed behind feeling thoroughly disconsolate. When they both headed for the Bakerloo Line, Kay's mood if anything dropped even lower but then they stopped, the man gave her a quick and very chaste hug and headed for the Southbound platform whilst she headed in the opposite direction. Kay gave a quick sigh of relief and followed her down to the platform.

The problem was that he now had to put his own acting abilities to the test and he was dealing with a professional. The indicator board read '*Harrow & Wealdstone 1 min*'. Not really enough time he thought, he would have to re-introduce himself on the train. Kay was standing two or three feet behind Em who was staring intently at her phone as the Bakerloo Line train pulled into the platform. The doors opened and a red-faced drunk lurched unsteadily off the train barging into Em, causing her to drop the phone which fell onto her foot, bounced onto the platform and then onto the track.

She stepped back searching for station staff, almost colliding with Kay whom she didn't at that moment recognise but there were no London Underground employees on the platform.

'Shit' she said, not for the first time in Kay's earshot.

The train pulled out leaving her and Kay the only people on the platform.

'Hold onto that' he said handing her his programme. Quickly he jumped down onto the track, retrieved her phone and with a smile handed it back to her.

She looked at him, screwed up her face as if trying to recall something from the depths of her memory.

'Kay?' she ventured.

Kay was overjoyed. She remembered him!

'That's me' he nodded with a smile.

'Are you some kind of guardian angel?'

'I think I might be' replied Kay, 'but I'm pleased to be at your service my lady' he said bowing his head.

Em laughed, 'Well I'm certainly grateful to you, again. Look, that's the second time you've dug me out of a scrape, I think I should owe you something'

Kay put his hand to his chin in a gesture suggesting deep thought, 'Can I ask you two simple favours which should see us even?'

'Okay' she replied somewhat hesitantly.

'Firstly, you can sign my programme'

'Of course', she looked at the programme while Kay handed her a pen, 'So now you know what I do'.

She quickly signed it '*To Kay with grateful thanks. Emma Silvester*'. Underneath she added two x's

'Only two?' said Kay.

She smiled and added another.

Just then, a large man with dreadlocks dressed in London Underground uniform walked past them, looked down the tunnel and then returned to speak to them.

'Did either of you see anybody get onto the track a couple of minutes ago?' he asked in a strong South London accent.

'No' said Kay with an air of complete innocence, 'nothing as exciting as that'.

The man gave them a vexed stare, shook his head, turned and walked back up the platform.

The two of them looked at each other and giggled quietly.

At that moment they heard the sound of an approaching train, accompanied by a gust of wind as it progressed noisily up the platform. They both got on and stood in the doorway.

'Where's home to you?' asked Kay.

'Right at this moment, Shepherd's Bush, near the market' she replied.

'So, you'll be changing at Paddington, right?' asked Kay 'I'm three stops before you at Baker Street. So, I haven't got long to ask my second favour'.

'Go on' she smiled.

'I would like to take you out to dinner' Kay announced.

'How do you know I don't have a loving partner waiting for me at home?' replied Em.

'I don't but if that's the case, I'll cry all the way home'.

'No need for tears,' said Em. 'There was someone but he wanted to keep me on a tight leash which, apart from being a general pain in the bum is hard to do with someone in my profession. So he had to go'.

'Okay you'll be working until Saturday. Sunday and Monday aren't good days to eat out anyway. What if we make it next Tuesday?'

'Fine by me' said Em. 'Oh, and hadn't we better exchange numbers?'

They'd finished swapping numbers just as the train drew into Baker Street. Kay gave her a little peck on the cheek with a 'see you next Tuesday' and they went their separate ways.

*

Kay turned up late for work on Thursday. Fortunately Tony was out on an appointment and Mike was too busy to take any notice.

As soon as Raj saw him he could see that something had happened. Kay had that cat that got the cream look about him.

'So you pulled?' said Raj.

'My lips are sealed' replied Kay with a smirk.

'You lucky bastard!' Raj retorted and then to the whole office, 'Kay's only gone and pulled a bloody actress'.

'Luck had nothing to do with it, it was obviously my innate charm and animal magnetism', Kay responded.

'What's her name, Lassie?' came a cry from Nick, one of Kay's colleagues on the Commercial section. The whole office descended into uproar.

'Are you sure you can handle this?', Raj leaned across the desk and whispered quietly to Kay, 'You'll be the envy of every male in this office' he paused, 'with the possible exception of James from Accounts. And can you imagine Tony's face when he finds out? His envy gene will go into overdrive'.

'I once dated an actor', said Gill from Motor, a plump, friendly woman now close to retirement, 'It took us all day to walk down the High Street. He had to stop and check his reflection in every shop window. He did a couple of adverts and then became a bus driver'.

Office banter was a way of life at Gresham & Bailey. It wasn't one of those places where everybody sat at their workstations, head down barely knowing the person at the next desk. There is little inherently interesting in insurance and for most people employed by Gresham & Bailey, the interplay between them made an otherwise miserable existence at least tolerable.

Maybe that was the problem, he hadn't the ambition to leave and go somewhere else, somewhere perhaps duller but with better prospects. His office friendships kept him in a job that he despised.

Chapter Five

Kay's mother opened the door.

'Hello darling' she said smothering him in a maternal embrace that was at one time both embarrassing and comforting.

Ruth Nettleton (née Weissman) was the daughter of a holocaust survivor and an East London shop assistant. Although close to death when the war ended, her father Immanuel (Manny) Weissman had made a miraculous recovery in time to be flown to England as one of what we now know as the Windermere Children. In truth he had received nothing more than ordinary civility from the Lakeland people that he met. The contrast however with the inhuman treatment at the hands of the Third Reich in Theresienstadt and other appalling places combined with the beautiful surroundings in which he found himself, transformed him into one of the most patriotic of Englishmen.

Manny wasted no time in getting married and starting a family. Although raised as an orthodox Jew, his horrific experiences during the war had wrung any trace of religion from his soul and Ruth (named after his mother who had died in Auschwitz) and her two younger sisters were brought up in various locations in West London, in a completely secular household.

Like her father, Ruth had married and started a family in her early twenties. Immediately after university and already four months pregnant she married a young mathematics graduate from Barnsley called Richard Nettleton. The assumption was made by many people that this was a shotgun wedding but they were wrong, Ruth and Richard had a real affection for one another and the pregnancy, although unplanned was very welcome.

With a small loan from their families and a larger one from the Leeds Permanent Building Society they bought a two bedroom flat in one of the less desirable parts of Amersham, a town drawn largely at random, Richard accepting that commuting to London would have to become a part of his life from thereon in.

In quick succession Ruth produced Paula then Kay. A third child, another boy, was stillborn which caused them much anguish. However, try as they might , it appeared that Ruth was unable to conceive again. But in an increasingly overcrowded world, two children were enough weren't they? Whatever spin they put on it though, the loss of their third child left a hole which they could not adequately fill.

Time passed, Ruth trained as a teacher, she and Richard moved house, first to a semi and then ten years later to a four bedroom detached house with a driveway and a quarter of an acre of garden. Then it happened, three days before her 44th birthday and long after she had given up all hope, Ruth found that she was pregnant again. For the next eight months she lived on her nerves remembering the tragic outcome of her last pregnancy. But in the end the child – a boy – was born fit and healthy. They named him Jack after Richard's father who had died of cancer the previous year.

*

Kay strode into the lounge and greeted his father with a warm hug. Immediately Jack began badgering him to go into the garden and play football but Kay stalled him with 'give me a minute Jack, I want to speak to Dad first'.

'How's work?' said Richard. Kay replied with a grimace, 'Fine if you like psychotic bosses, Dickensian working conditions and unreasonable customers '.

'So going well then' replied Richard with a chuckle.

His mother came in, 'and is there anyone special in your life Kay?'

'No, not really Mum' he replied but he knew that she would pick up on every slight nuance in his voice and his reply had told her what she wanted to know.

'So who is she' Ruth persisted.

'I told you, there's no one' responded Kay knowing he was fooling nobody least of all his mother. She gave him a quizzical look and dropped the subject, at least for the time being. Ruth had liked Vicky and was very upset when she and Kay were no longer a couple. Kay knew that she had secretly stayed in touch with his ex and the two women would occasionally chat on the phone about things in general, but mostly about him.

It had become a family ritual that once a month Kay would visit his parents for Sunday lunch. His sister could no longer join them as she was busy producing a family with her Kiwi husband in far-away Wanganui.

Over lunch Kay and Richard talked animatedly about football, in part about the season that had just finished, with United winning the title ahead of Liverpool and Chelsea. But more they bemoaned the way that too much money was ruining the game. Richard, who had himself been a useful left winger, held that too many foreign players were stunting the development of home-grown talent. Kay countered with the argument that there was nothing other than the natural insularity of the British preventing young players from plying their trade in Europe.

After lunch, Kay was finally persuaded to kick a football around the garden with Jack who like his father and brother was beginning to show some aptitude for the game, an aptitude that would see him playing league football by his twenty first birthday. At the age of twelve he already had a vicious shot on him which made keeping goal a hazardous occupation even for somebody with sharp reflexes.

Kay's mind was, of course, elsewhere. He had arranged to meet Em at The Dove in Hammersmith, a pub that he knew had the right ambiance for a first date, with the intention of dining later at an intimate restaurant he knew in Kensington. They had communicated via text as Kay wanted to save conversation for next Tuesday. Not that he was concerned about running out of chat, he knew enough of Em to suspect that this was unlikely to happen but he wanted to keep the powder dry on his best stories.

He stayed at his parents' for tea, discussing politics and watching a little television. As if he had planned it, the Sunray Shampoo commercial appeared which made him smile. He did consider telling his mother everything; that in two days' time he had a date with the young woman in the advert. But it was too far-fetched, she would never believe him and it might even cause her to worry about his mental state. So he kept his own counsel, revealing all would have to wait for another occasion.

Chapter Six

Tuesday dawned blustery and intermittently wet with a procession of heavy cumulus clouds racing across the sky. Not an auspicious start to the day Kay thought. He had taken the opportunity to take both Tuesday and Wednesday as holiday, and although the second day might have reflected a degree of optimism, it also meant that if things didn't go well he had a day to recover before facing the curiosity of his colleagues. It was not unknown for Tony to phone employees irrespective of their holidays, so he made sure his work mobile was turned off and thrown into a pile of dirty washing in the corner of his bedroom. With singular optimism, he made sure his wallet contained more than just money…

Almost immediately, he found that he was unable to concentrate on anything much, even the basics of life such as getting his breakfast. After an hour of pacing up and down, he decided that to settle his nerves he needed to give himself a focus, so he put his golf bag in the car and headed for a driving range ten miles away, near Hemel Hempstead.

There was much about golf that irritated him, its petty rules on what you could and could not wear, the general reactionary nature of many clubs and their tin-pot hierarchies. He just liked hitting balls and wasn't bad at it considering the sporadic nature of his visits to a golf course.

He hit three hundred balls that morning, most reasonably well although the odd few did sail out of the confines of the range when he either sliced or hooked them. He found though that the activity had calmed him down and he was now much more able to concentrate on the world around him that afternoon than he had been in the morning.

Looking at himself in the mirror before he left home, he was convinced that he had got it right, an open-necked shirt and casual trousers. Smart but not too smart. He wondered what Em would be wearing. So far, he had only seen her in jeans and a tee shirt which suited her well but clearly there would be other things in her wardrobe.

The time of their rendezvous was to be quarter past seven and to give himself plenty of time he caught the 17.13 from Chorleywood. As it happened, he was glad he did, as due to an 'incident at King's Cross', the train stopped in the tunnel between Finchley Road and Baker Street for a full ten minutes before crawling into the station and unwontedly terminating there. If he had had a heartbeat monitor, it is fair to say that during this hiatus in proceedings his pulse count would have gone through the roof.

He arrived at The Dove at five to seven and immediately ordered himself a pint of London Pride, a standard go-to beer that he had ordered many hundreds of times before. He didn't want to drink anything too strong and he didn't want to drink it too quickly, thus necessitating another pint which would result in frequent trips to the Gents throughout the evening. Ideally, she would arrive when he was half way through his pint indicating that he had got there in good time to meet her but had not been too eager.

Understandably he had a keen eye on the clock. Seven o'clock came and went, a minute past, two, three… twelve, thirteen, fourteen. He hadn't expected her to arrive dead on the dot but when seven twenty arrived he began to feel a little anxious. By seven twenty-five his eye was almost permanently on his watch.

Shortly after seven thirty he became aware of a commotion in the alleyway outside and above it all he could hear Em's clear voice say, 'Just go, you've caused enough trouble already!'

Kay got up and rushed to the door just as Em entered looking rather calmer than he had expected.

'What was that about?' said Kay.

'Just a bad smell from my past' replied Em, 'don't let it worry you'.

Kay thought for a minute. If it didn't concern her why should he let it concern him? So he took a deep breath and said, 'You look stunning!'.

And she did.

He was delighted to see that rather than slavishly following fashion she was wearing clothes that suited her to a tee. He would have been lying if he'd said he hadn't noticed her breasts on the two previous occasions they had met but the red and white hooped off the shoulder blouse she was wearing emphasised them deliciously. Kay had to make a conscious effort to stop himself from staring.

Em however had clearly noticed. 'You approve?' she said with a twinkle in her eye.

Kay felt himself blushing. But her outfit did seem to indicate something - she had made an effort to dress as if the occasion meant something to her and that it wasn't just as the repayment of a favour.

He bought her a glass of Sauvignon Blanc and they chatted lightly about music – their tastes turned out to be fairly similar, both, for example, loved the addictive, uncompromising alto of (the soon to be late) Amy Winehouse - and about ridiculous situations that had occurred at Gresham & Bailey which made Em laugh.

At eight-fifteen the cab which Kay had taken the precaution of ordering arrived and they left for the second part of their evening at a small Italian restaurant just off Kensington High Street. Em would have no more than two antipasti because, as she explained 'when you're not very big, a normal size meal could turn you into a balloon overnight'. For his part, Kay ordered pan-seared scallops followed by tagliatelle carbonara washed down with a bottle of Frascati.

'Other than you're drop-dead gorgeous and you're a great actor, I know nothing about you'.

'Now you'll make me blush' Em replied with a hint of irony, 'but I'll take the compliments'.

She continued 'There really isn't much to tell, I've lived most of my life in Acton. My Dad died when I was three'.

'I'm sorry'

'Don't be, he was a wrong 'un' she went on 'Had he lived I still wouldn't have seen him much, he spent most of his life in The Scrubs. But my Mum's a diamond.

As a kid, me, my Mum and my sister Ethel…'

'Ethel!' laughed Kay, 'If our families have got anything in common, it's that they shouldn't be allowed to name kids!'

'They're just family names from Trinidad that couldn't be left behind, or so my Mum says but I've always wished that I was called something else.
The first few years we spent on the twelfth floor of a tower block in South Acton. You've probably seen it, the BBC used it for '*Only Fools and Horses*'. My most vivid memory is that the lift stank of wee.

And then after a few months of living in pretty minging private accommodation in Hammersmith, the council allocated us a little house in East Acton where my Mum still lives'.

'So how did you get into acting?'

'A good question. The honest answer is I really haven't a clue. I went to several auditions for child parts when I was small – I know I'm not much bigger now' she said with a smile 'but I never got any of them. Then in the last year at school I landed the leading role in the school play. Eventually I applied for a scholarship to RADA and amazingly I got in'.

As she spoke, Kay began to feel immense envy for this intelligent and playful young woman with a fledgling career doing what she loved. Even the most successful businessman would say that given the chance he would rather play in the FA Cup Final, Wimbledon, Lords or even *Hamlet* at The Royal

Shakespeare Theatre rather than the high-powered, if mundane, career that fate had handed him.

'Well that's my story. Now who are you and why do you keep turning up?'

Kay proceeded to relate the story of his life so far and when he got to his abortive footballing career, a tear appeared in his eye and ran down his cheek. It was the first time he had shown his feelings to anybody, even his parents, about the cruel turn of fate that had wrecked his ambition for the future. Unbelievably, she reached out across the table and gently touched his hand, 'Yes it figures, I could see you as a footballer'. The brief silence that hung in the air following this statement said much.

He looked at her and changing the subject said quietly, 'When I first saw you on the train that time, I thought there was something different about you. Somehow you just didn't look as if you did any of the jobs people in London normally do. I couldn't see you sitting behind a desk sending tedious emails to tedious people'. And changing tone, 'Wow, I've dated an actress, that's really cool!'

'It can be far from glamorous' she said with a smile, 'Smelly, cramped dressing rooms, directors with an ego the size of a planet, revolting old men three times my age with wandering hands who get away with it because they're 'stars'. But I wouldn't do anything else, it's my life'.

Compared to this, Kay's life since his injury seemed trite and inconsequential but he continued with an abridged form of the story. When he got to the bit about Vicky she asked the inevitable question, 'Did you love her?'

'I'm really not sure, it's not even as if we grew apart. I guess we were just too similar from day one. Having a lot in common is not all it's cracked up to be'. And then after a pause he added, 'She's currently living with a solicitor in Barnes'.

Kay could feel the atmosphere of the evening getting heavy so he began to tell her a string of terrible jokes. He wasn't sure whether she was being polite but her laugh was an intoxicant far more potent than the Italian wine they'd been drinking. So, he dredged his memory banks for ever more dreadful quips and one-liners. What surprised him was that she responded with any number of her own which were rather more risqué than the ones he was prepared to offer on such a brief acquaintance. In fact some were downright dirty and almost, but not quite, made Kay blush.

At just after eleven o'clock they left the restaurant with the intention of catching a cab on Kensington High Street. They had walked no more than ten yards down the road when he put his hand on her shoulder and carefully turned her to face him. They kissed, a long passionate kiss. Seizing his opportunity he put his hand under her blouse and could feel her smooth, taut midriff. His hand continued on to feel her bra with the promise of much greater joys within. She wriggled a little and carefully removed his hand. 'Later' she said.

'Will there be a later?' he replied, desperately hoping that there would.

She looked him directly in the eyes and said 'If you want there to be. I don't turn into a pumpkin at midnight'.

'Now let me check my diary... um... yes, I think I'm free,' came his reply.

'Well you're in luck, my flatmate's away tonight so we've got the whole place to ourselves'.

These words were music to his ears. But they also brought with them some concerns for Kay. A beautiful woman like this must have had many lovers before. How would he compare to them? Would she find him attractive stripped of his clothes? Would he be too eager? All these things and many more went through Kay's mind and cast, not a large cloud but a few cirrus-like wisps across his sky.

They walked up to the High Street with his arm round her shoulder, still sharing the occasional kiss. After five minutes or so they managed to hail a cab which took them back to her flat in Frithville Gardens, a stone's throw from Shepherd's Bush Market. Although not familiar with this particular street, the area was well-known to Kay, being very close to Loftus Road, the home of Queen's Park Rangers. He recalled sadly that he had spent much time here in his early teenage years. Despite the dark, Kay could see that the street mostly consisted of three-storey Victorian terraced houses with small front gardens, now mostly concreted over and intimate little doorways. Here and there, were uninspired later developments, presumably built immediately after the war to fill gaps where Hitler had done his worst.

Kay was pleased when Em took out her keys and headed up the short path to one of the former.

When they had got inside and shut the door behind them, they fell upon each other. Kay was constantly telling himself, 'Be calm, take it easy, you've got all the time in the world'. His animal instincts were however driving him forward at a furious pace but for the moment, his head had gained the upper hand over his heart.

Still holding his hand, Em led him up to the top floor, inserted the key in the lock, and entered the flat. She immediately turned on the light.

'Ouch!' said Kay.

'It's just for a second,' said Em, 'but I need to see where I'm going'.

The corridor of the flat could be described as typical of its type, walls covered with anaglypta, daubed with magnolia paint, telephone wires haphazardly nailed to the skirting board and painted over umpteen times. A purple lampshade that had been cheap when it was bought, maybe twenty years ago hung from the ceiling.

Taking his hand again she opened the door and led him into a small room, which turned out to be her bedroom. She switched on a bedside lamp containing nothing more than a 40 watt bulb. The room was covered in replica posters, mostly of films – *Breakfast at Tiffany's, La Dolce Vita, Casablanca.* There was also one of Bob Marley. Nothing that one could call new but all indisputably classics. There was a chair and a desk covered in what Kay rightly assumed to be film scripts. The bed (which he was surprised to notice was only a single) had been made hurriedly rather than carefully but it would undoubtedly serve its purpose.

The animal in him was beginning to gain the upper hand now and he pulled her towards him, kissed her on the lips, their tongues meeting sensuously. Again, he put his hand under her blouse and this time received no resistance. Kay had a friend who claimed to be able to undo bra straps with one hand in under two seconds but this was a skill he had never mastered. Tutting kindly and rolling her eyes, Em said 'Let me do it for you. You're all fingers and thumbs'. With both hands she reached behind her back and undid the now superfluous item of lingerie.

He could feel her breasts drop slightly as they were released from their lacy prison. He fondled them eagerly and ran his tongue round each nipple in turn. At the same time Em was undoing his shirt. Once this garment had been discarded, he bent down to remove his own shoes and socks – he had the presence of mind to realise that there could be nothing less sexy than standing completely naked except for the pair of Dennis the Menace socks that Jack had given him last Christmas.

Within a few seconds they were both naked. Clothed, he had thought her beautiful but naked she was nothing short of exquisite. He immediately noticed that her body was free from tattoos. Rare for a woman of her age he thought, but it immediately occurred to him that no sensible actor would ever sully their skin in such a way. Taking a step back to absorb the full beauty of her form, he observed that she still boasted a full crop of pubic hair. Again, he thought this unusual but it suited him fine, he never could see the point of spending time removing what was, after all, a natural embellishment to the human body.

He knelt down to gently kiss and caress the neat triangle of hair that covered her mons pubis. The inevitable happened. Not one but two hairs came away in his mouth. He got to his feet and made a wry smile while he attempted, not altogether successfully to remove them. Em began to giggle. Her giggle turned into a laugh which communicated itself to Kay. She laughed even more when she noticed the effect that Kay's own laughter was having on his erection. He took a short step forward, tripped over a shoe and the two of them collapsed in a laughing, giggling heap on the bed.

The sudden outburst of laughter was the ideal cure for Kay's first-night nerves. Had Shepherd's Bush been the sort of place where the inhabitants were wont to keep poultry, Kay and Em would have made love three times before the cock crowed. And it was good sex too. Her response told him that Em had enjoyed it as much as he had. He was as certain as he could be that she wasn't faking.

But he was wrong about one thing. She did have a tattoo. On her right buttock was the representation of a butterfly. 'A small tortoiseshell' said Kay, 'Whoever did this was quite an artist. Perfect in every detail, as is the canvas'. He bent down and kissed it.

'My one indulgence,' replied Em. 'Besides, it's an identification test,' and then a second later, 'You may be pleased to know you're the first to pass'.

'So I get to see you again?'

'Hmm, let me think about that... Of course you do, you silly boy. If that's what you want but I've had a great time. It was brilliant but I could really do with some sleep now'. She stretched provocatively. Had his ardour not been totally spent, this would have spurred him on to further action but as it was, he just lay down and fell fast asleep.

Despite the two of them being squashed into a single bed, Kay didn't wake up again until ten, with Em fast asleep next to him wearing the Mona Lisa smile that had so captivated him on their first meeting.

In countless films the hero gets up to make breakfast for his lady after a good night of fun and frolics and who was Kay to buck the trend? He crept silently out of bed and still unclothed found his way to the kitchen after first having paid an essential visit to the bathroom. He looked down at his penis. It was a little red but had performed sterling service over the last night and was very much in need of a rest.

There wasn't much food in the flat but he did find some eggs, half a loaf of bread and a tiny quantity of cooking oil. So it would have to be fried eggs on toast.

While he was frying the eggs, Em, still naked, crept up behind him and put her hand over his eyes. In so doing she pressed her body hard against Kay's back.

'Any more of that, young lady and I'll be frying my dick for breakfast as well'.

Em turned him round and kissed him on the neck. 'Ah, poor thing' she said looking at his member, 'he looks sore. Let me kiss him better'.

'That's actually going to make him worse,' said Kay but it was too late. She took his penis in her left hand and planted a big wet kiss on the shaft.

Just at that moment there was the sound of a key in the lock followed by the creaking of a door. It was Em's flat-mate Jodi. In a panic Kay looked around and caught sight of an apron hanging behind the kitchen door. Hastily he put it on.

Jodi strolled into the kitchen and with seemingly wide-eyed innocence surveyed the scene; Em standing completely naked and a strange man with a fish slice in his hand wearing her floral-print apron and seemingly nothing else.

'Right you two,' she said with her hands over her eyes, 'I'm going to go back outside, count to a hundred and when I come back in, I expect to see you fully clothed'. With that she strode back outside and shut the door.

Kay and Em looked at each other and giggled.

'One, two, three…' came the voice from outside the flat. With all due haste they ran into Em's bedroom and began looking for their clothes. The process was hindered by the fact that every time Kay found an article of Em's attire he hid it, meaning that when she did leave the room she was missing her bra (it was inside the pillow case) and one sock.

'Ninety eight, ninety nine, one hundred,' came Jodi's voice. 'I'm coming ready or not'.

As promised, Jodi entered the flat and marched into the kitchen.

'Hello Em,' she said, 'Who's this? Are you going to introduce me?'

'Hello Jodi,' said Em like the good actress she was, 'this is my friend Kay. Kay-Jodi, Jodi-Kay'.

'Charmed I'm sure,' said Kay, ostentatiously kissing Jodi's hand.

From that moment the three of them carried on as if Take One had never happened.

Chapter Seven

Kay's arrival at the office the following morning mirrored the previous Thursday, even the quips were similar.

'How was Lassie?' asked Nick.

'Christ,' thought Kay, 'You did that one last week'.

'Very well thank you,' he grudgingly replied.

Raj arrived ten minutes later and immediately looked at Kay, raising one eyebrow in the manner of Roger Moore. Kay gave him the thumbs up sign with both hands.

'Enough said,' was Raj's retort.

There is a curious protocol among men with regard to discussing sexual encounters which works in inverse proportion to their importance. One-night stands and dead-end holiday romances can be dissected in minute detail but as soon as a relationship appears to have legs, discussion becomes distinctly muted. Sex with long-term partners and wives is only ever alluded to in the vaguest terms.

At lunchtime, Kay managed to slip out for a beer with Raj.

'I'm guessing from your demeanour that you've had a good couple of days,' said Raj.

'Oh yes,' replied Kay, 'I'm seeing her again on Friday'.

'Wow that good! Mind you she's a cracking looking bird. I do envy you Kay old son'.

'Bird… bird?!' You realise you're referring to one of the country's finest young actresses…'

'Who's clearly got a screw loose to be dating you,' interjected Raj, 'Anyway, be careful, Tony's been in a foul mood these last couple of days and the fact that he now knows you've pulled a real popsy who's been on TV hasn't improved his mood one iota. Ever since the third Mrs. Bailey walked out on him last year he's got in a real strop when anybody mentions their wife or girlfriend. I should take it easy for the foreseeable if I were you'.

In fact his marital disharmony was not the only thing affecting Tony's mood at that time. Following the subprime mortgage crisis and the collapse of Lehman Brothers, G & B's business was down dramatically, perhaps by as much as 30%. Companies were watching every penny and seeking to cut out the middle-man wherever possible. This did not help his notoriously short temper. On one occasion Kay walked past his office and heard:

'I'm so sorry George, I'll make sure you get an answer by the end of the day. Somebody's going to get their arse kicked for this!'

Kay had heard this sort of thing before. Somebody was indeed going to get their arse kicked. That person turned out to be Kay, at least at first.

Tony Bailey finished the conversation with, 'We'll have to have another round of golf, George. Trust me, I'll sort it out. Bye George, bye'. As soon as the exchange ended, the door to Tony's office flew open and with a volume only otherwise experienced on the tarmac at major international airports he shouted,

'Kay, where's the fucking Gainsborough Developments file?!'

'Bollocks' thought Kay. He went to the filing system. Nothing.

He searched several files in each direction from 'Frinton Whole Foods' to 'Harris Brothers (Construction) Ltd.'. Still nothing.

'Sorry Tony, I can't find it' he replied defensively.

'What do you mean you can't fucking find it?'

'I can't find it. It isn't in the filing system'.

'Everybody look on your desks. I need this bastard file now!' bellowed Tony.

And everybody from Mike Hancock to the office junior on the Household section who had only been there three days looked on their desks. Still no file.

Then Kay remembered. He marched straight past Tony, into his office, moved several piles of paper and under a three week old copy of '*The Financial Times*' he retrieved a red file marked 'Gainsborough Developments'. In it was a copy of an e-mail dated twenty seven days earlier and marked 'urgent'.

'How the fuck did that get there?' said Tony

'You told me to put it there, something about you wanting to arrange a round of golf with George Hyland'.

Kay expected no thanks and got none. His boss just brushed past him and slammed the door. Kay smirked and wondered how good Tony was at kicking his own arse.

Chapter Eight

Kay had spent the rest of that Wednesday in West London. He and Em again caught the train to Hammersmith and strolled hand in hand along the river before returning to Frithville Gardens to make love once, in fact twice, more.

It was later that evening that they had their first disagreement.

'So I guess you're 'resting' now,' said Kay, 'what do you do to earn money when you haven't got work for weeks or months?'

'Usually I find work in local pubs or shops and I've even been a life model at the Slade,' replied Em.

'You mean an artistic stripper'.

Kay realised he'd crossed a line as soon as he had said it.

'Don't take the piss out of me Kay. At least I've got the balls to do what it takes to follow my passion. Unlike some people I could mention'.

'You know what happened to me,' he replied. 'That was my passion'.

'But you dwell on it, you do a job that you hate, writing off half your life. Find another passion and follow that'.

After a second or two, Kay broke the silence. 'I'm sorry, that was very thoughtless of me'.

'Most of your life has been a doddle. You were brought up in a comfortable home and had everything you could reasonably want. If things went wrong you could always go running to Mummy and Daddy. It wasn't like that for me. Finding ways of making ends meet has always been a necessity not a stupid game.'

Another silence. Em broke it this time.

'And I'm sorry too. I can see how much football meant to you but there was a grain of truth in there somewhere. Just take it as advice from a friend'.

'A friend?'

'A bit more than that then'.

They had agreed to meet at Baker Street station on Friday after work, a place which despite being among the scruffier of London Underground's stations had already acquired mythical status in their relationship. The plan was that they would then catch the train to Chorleywood and spend the weekend at Kay's flat.

Kay was running late and Em was already there, waiting for him under the old train departure board when he arrived. She looked at her watch and tutted.

'Sorry, I had some work to finish off,' he said. The next Monday for Kay would consist of an all day visit to butter up the narcissistic Managing Director of a waste processing company in Dunstable and he was preparing the ground. Em had of course been right, this was not the sort of thing of which dreams were made. But she didn't seem to bear him a grudge for his lateness and the journey to Chorleywood went as smoothly as it could.

Chorleywood is a curious place. It can't make up its mind whether it is a large village or a small town. The shopping centre is mostly post-war and mainly concentrates on retail. There are no pubs but there are restaurants and cafés. On weekday evenings however, it does tend to be quiet, if not entirely deserted. Em took one look at the place and said, 'what the hell do you find to do here?'.

'It's not what's here' replied Kay, 'it's what's round and about; the countryside, wildlife, golf courses, country pubs. That sort of thing. It's the essence of England'.

Em shrugged.

Kay understood that Em's life experience had been almost entirely urban and it might take her some time to adapt to his ways in the same way that he would have to adapt to hers. For his part, although he liked spending time in large towns and cities with their obvious attractions, he always felt a little hemmed in and couldn't wait to re-charge his batteries somewhere where life was less pressured.

He had made great efforts to tidy his flat but he could not disguise the fact that it was a rather dreary single bedroom apartment over a women's hairdressers. Em made no comment. She seemed to be aware that this was just a transit stop and not his forever home. It would do *pro tem* but he got the vibe that it would certainly not suffice if he wanted her to move in with him.

Again he took her out for a meal, this time to a pub in Sarratt but as that was a few miles away and he had to drive, his alcohol intake was severely curtailed. Holding hands across the table, Em looked at him and said, 'Please don't take this the wrong way but you arriving in my life has been so sudden that I really feel all at sea. I'm just not sure I know you yet. You've told me about yourself but I can't say I truly understand anything about you. Until I've met some of your friends, perhaps even your family and seen the places you hang out I really won't be able to get you into context. For all I know, your friends might have pointy tails, horns growing out of their heads and go around carrying oversized toasting forks. Don't forget some of my ancestors were slaves, we have a natural suspicion about people'.

'Well you might just be in luck, next Friday we're having a party after work to celebrate the twentieth anniversary of G & B. Wives and girlfriends are invited'.

*

The following morning, Kay took Em to Combe Hill where the Chilterns descend into the Vale of Aylesbury. This provides as good a vista as anywhere in the Home Counties and on a clear day the visitor has views over the three adjoining counties. It is said that if you travel due east from here, the first place you come to with a higher elevation is in the Ural Mountains.

It was late spring and all around them nature was in its pomp. Robins, wrens and blackbirds were in full voice and chiffchaffs appeared to be singing their monotonous little song from every tree top. The best of the bluebells and primroses had now passed but there were still examples to be found here and there while in the hedgerows, hawthorn and crab apple were in full bloom.

Kay had retained his love of nature and amongst other things was now a qualified bird-ringer. Em had seldom been to such a place before but his infectious enthusiasm for his surroundings communicated itself to her and she clearly found the location enchanting. With his knowledge of nature, Kay was well placed to answer her questions concerning what she could see around her.

'What are those big birds circling above us,' she asked.

'Red kites. If you had come here twenty years ago you wouldn't have seen even one'.

'I've heard of them but I don't think I've ever seen one. They're much bigger than I thought'.

Just then, a cackling sound, not that far away, caused them to look up.

'What was that?'

'A green woodpecker.' Let's see if we can find it'.

Creeping through the straggly grassland they were rewarded with a good view of a large green and red bird which eventually caught sight of them, laughed and flew away.

'Fantastic! You'll turn me into a bird watcher!' Reaching up, she kissed him, 'You see, you do still have passions'.

At Combe Hill there is a tall memorial to the fallen men of Buckinghamshire who fought in the Second Boer War. Sitting at its base, they persuaded a friendly looking stranger to take their photograph.

'I'm not sure I like this, smacks of colonialism, the British Empire and all that'.

'You've got a British as well as an African half Em, and these people weren't fighting Africans. They were fighting the Boers who went on to create apartheid'.

'Well it's a shame they didn't make a better job of it then. In fact my African half isn't a half at all,' Em replied authoritatively, 'First of all there are as many people of Indian descent in Trinidad. Added to that the slave masters used to take liberties with their female slaves. I'm probably no more than 25% African'.

'And I'm a quarter Jewish. Imagine if we had kids, what a mixture they'd be. And there's probably Irish and Scottish to add to the mixture. But I'm getting a bit ahead of myself there…'

Em replied with a look that Kay couldn't fathom. Did it say, 'Play your cards right?' or 'In your dreams'. Kay wasn't sure but he filed that look in his memory banks and referred to it often over the years.

*

Kay didn't consider himself much of a chef but that evening he cooked Em a passable chicken risotto that seemed to hit the spot. The bottle of prosecco may have played its part too…

Lying in bed that night after another very satisfying evening of pleasure, Kay turned to Em and said softly, 'you remember when I met you on Waterloo Station'.

'Yes'

'Did it never occur to you why I was there?'

'Well, not really. I guess I just assumed you were there to see the play'.

'That's not even a tenth of the story. That time I dropped you off in Watford, I felt I'd missed a massive opportunity. I fancied you like crazy but by the time I'd got my thoughts in order, you'd gone'.

'I was fully expecting you to say something, at least take my number. But it wasn't the best time anyway, I was quite heavily involved with somebody then who turned out to be a complete jerk'.

Kay leaned up on his elbow and looked her in the face, 'I would probably have put it in that corner of my mind marked 'missed opportunities' and then slowly forgotten about you. Until I saw you in Eastenders…'

Em laughed, 'That was one afternoon's work. I just had to drink a glass of water, pretend it was wine and chat inanely to another extra called Joe. A really nice guy but unfortunately for me, he was gay'.

'And then there was the Sunray Shampoo advert. You just kept haunting me'.

'That was good money but I spent the entire day either soaking wet or under a hair drier. I never get the sexy jobs where they send you off to the Mediterranean for three weeks to film a holiday commercial'.

'So I decided, sod it,' continued Kay, 'I'm going to find out who she is if it kills me. I eventually got your name from a theatrical message board. I just posted 'Who's the girl in the Sunray Shampoo advert,' and after a couple of weeks somebody replied, 'Her name is Emma Silvester' but that's all they said'.

'Ha ha, that would be my Mum,' interjected Em, 'She's a real one for promoting her younger daughter's acting career. I'm actually dead lucky she didn't continue, '… but her real name's Maude".

'And from there I tracked you down to the National Theatre. Quite a jump from shampoo'.

'Yes it is, isn't it? I only got it at the last moment. The actor who was originally pencilled in for the part got pregnant and had to pull out'.

Kay laughed, 'So if her partner had pulled out, she wouldn't have had to!'

Em slapped him playfully, 'Theatre is real hard work. Long hours and late nights but there's a real camaraderie between the members of the cast and crew'.

The following day they went to Marlow to sit by the Thames and watch the world go by. Em had an audition on Monday and needed to read the script, so Kay drove her back to Shepherd's Bush in the early evening. Nonetheless they agreed to meet up on Tuesday and then again for the G & B party on the Friday.

*

As it turned out Kay stayed over at Em's on Tuesday night although the confines of a single bed and her nakedness in such close proximity meant that neither of them got much sleep. Kay had therefore to go to work on Wednesday bleary eyed and in the same clothes as the day before. His colleagues at work noticed but other than Raj who simply looked at him and shook his head, made no comment.

Tony had booked the whole of a small restaurant in Greek Street for Friday's party and to give him his due, this was going to cost a tidy sum. Food was to be in the form of a rather upmarket buffet and the drinks, including a large quantity of vintage champagne, were to be free all night. Not everybody who worked for G & B was looking forward to the event. Jayne Bentley had never taken to Tony, 'I just don't like the way he looks at me sometimes. Just call it my intuition. I think he's really creepy,' so it was no surprise when she announced that there was no way she was going to attend. She had however agreed that she and her partner Dan, who played tight-head prop for Richmond, would meet the others in Soho after the event.

Kay met Em just round the corner in the Nellie Dean in Dean Street. He thought it fair that Em should make up her own mind about Tony so other than telling her that he could be a little over-familiar with women, said little about him.

The party was due to start at seven thirty but in order to let the place fill up a little before their arrival, they didn't leave the pub until nearly eight.

As soon as Em entered the room, it was obvious that Tony was taking a keen interest in her. He strode over to where they were standing, 'Can you explain to me what a beautiful girl like you sees in a bozo like this?' he said, pointing at Kay and chortling in a self-satisfied way. Kay gave Em a glance which said, 'Yes I know he's a pratt but he *is* my boss,' and headed for the food table.

'Oh, I think he's rather sweet,' said Em, 'and...' she looked from left to right as if to check that nobody was listening, then beckoned with her finger for Tony to come closer and whispered, '... he's got the most enormous willy!'. She then indicated with her hands fisherman style, something between thirty five and fifty centimetres.

Tony stepped back in amazement, for once completely lost for words. Em casually turned her back on him and strolled over to join Kay at the buffet table.

'What did you say?'

'I just told him you were hung like a donkey. It seemed to nonplus him. I can't think why!' replied Em with a giggle.

'And why did you say that? He'll be following me into the khazi every time I go just to check if you're right. Besides...' he whispered quietly, 'he'd be terribly disappointed'.

'Well, the guy's a complete dickhead. I could see him mentally undressing me as soon as I came into the room and then to insult you the way he did, I just thought he was out of order. I know he's your boss but sometimes these people need taking down a notch or two. And as for your willy, it's perfect, don't let anybody tell you it isn't'.

'I'm not sure how to take that.' said Kay trying to keep a straight face.

They were shortly joined by Raj and his girlfriend Kate. His parents were first generation immigrants from Gujarat and much to their chagrin Raj had let it be known that the choice of a life partner would be made by him and him alone and in that search no-one would be excluded. Hence Kate, being descended from East Anglian farming stock was as Anglo-Saxon as they come with a peach-like complexion, blue eyes and pale brown hair.

Addressing Kay but looking directly at Em, Raj said with great enthusiasm, 'do you mind if I kiss your lady friend Kay?'.

'Of course not, as long as I can kiss yours'.

'Two reasons for this request,' continued Raj. 'Firstly I like kissing beautiful women. You can't fault my logic so far'.

'Agreed'.

'And secondly,' addressing Em directly, 'whatever you said to Tony has for the first time in living memory, completely shut him up. He hasn't uttered a peep since you spoke to him'.

Moving along the display of fine foods that the restaurant had prepared, the four of them were joined by other members of the staff. As ever on these sort of occasions, it was illuminating to contrast the people you knew at work with their partners whom you seldom, if ever, saw. Nick for example, all mouth and trousers in the office had a large and domineering wife, whose presence completely changed his personality. At work he had an opinion on everything but this evening with his wife in tow, he wouldn't say 'boo!'

After the party had gradually petered out about ten o'clock the four of them went off to meet Jayne and Dan in a night club in Old Compton Street where they continued drinking until two a.m. Pressed on why she hadn't attended the party, Jayne would only say, 'I've heard rumours,' and despite the amount of alcohol consumed refused to enlarge on the topic.

By the end of the evening, none of them could see straight but, if nothing else, Em now had some idea of the people with whom Kay normally associated. It seemed unlikely however that she would have anything more than a hazy recollection of the occasion.

Chapter Nine

Summer 2010

It soon became clear to Em and Kay that their domestic
arrangements were far from satisfactory. Em's bedroom in her
flat share contained only a single bed while Kay's flat in
Chorleywood was too far from the action and would be
impractical if she was offered a role in a West End or other
London production.

As it happened their hand was forced when Em obtained work
as understudy in *Anne Boleyn* at The Globe Theatre replacing an
actress who was leaving for personal reasons. She was not due to
start rehearsals for another three weeks but from then on it
would no longer be feasible for her to come to Chorleywood at
weekends. They therefore agreed that they would look for
alternative accommodation together somewhere near Em's
existing flat. After a short search they both moved into an
apartment, very much like Em's previous one, not 400 yards
away in Coverdale Road.

All through that summer they laughed and made love. Copious
quantities of both. In fact it became a standing joke between
them that Tracey Emin's bed had nothing on theirs.

One day, Em said, 'Don't you think it's about time we met each other's families'.

Totally absorbed by the football he was watching on TV, Kay replied, 'Yes whatever,' and carried on watching the game.

So it was that the following Monday morning, Em informed Kay that in roughly nine hours' time, he was going to meet her mother. 'Why?' asked Kay, 'I don't remember agreeing to that'.

'You did, on Saturday,'

'Well I don't remember'.

Em sighed. Kay shrugged but raised no objections. 'So be it,' he thought.

*

Patience Silvester - she called herself Pat - was very young looking to be the mother of two women in their twenties. She was of roughly the same height as her daughter and men still stopped and looked when she walked down the street. For the last six years she had shared her life with Jim Lascelles, a tall, likeable Jamaican, five years her junior, who made his living as a car mechanic. But to describe Jim as 'just' a car mechanic was like describing Van Gogh as 'just' an artist or Sir Christopher Wren as 'just' an architect. Cars were Jim's life and outside their house had, over time, been parked a succession of 'hot' Fords built from the 1960s through to the 1990s – an Escort RS2000, a Sierra RS Cosworth, a lethal Capri into which he had shoehorned an American Small Block V8 and for a few weeks a 1969 Mustang with a huge 6.4 litre engine.

Jim and Pat had a cat and dog relationship marked by loud slanging matches and passionate makings up. So, their unfortunate neighbours couldn't win. It was either shouts and screams as the two of them argued hammer and tongs, or the persistent squeaking of their over-stressed bed springs. Despite the noise however, the two of them got the reputation of being happy to help anybody at any time, particularly when babysitting was required or when a car would not start.

The Old Oak Estate where Pat and Jim lived was one of the larger public sector housing estates in West London. For the first forty or so years of its existence it went largely unnoticed unless you happened to live in or near it. Then, on August 12th 1966 that all changed.

The inaccurately named Shepherd's Bush Murders hit the national headlines that evening when it was reported that three policemen had been murdered in Braybrook Street on the northern edge of the estate by the notorious criminal Harry Roberts and his two accomplices, John Duddy and John Witney. Duddy and Witney were soon apprehended but Roberts kept the press, the police and a fearful public on high alert as he went on the run. For three months he kept the nation's doors double locked before being arrested while camping in woodland near Bishops Stortford.

This was, of course, many years before the Silvester family moved in but people of a certain age still characterised the Old Oak Estate as the place where those three unfortunate policemen were murdered and gave it a wide berth. In truth, there were far worse places to live and Pat and her two young daughters were grateful for the comparatively well-equipped house with a small garden they had been allocated in Mellitus Street.

When Kay was introduced to Pat, he could immediately see where Em had got her good looks and said as much.

'I like this one,' Pat said looking at Em. Kay had been expecting a Caribbean accent but what he got was pure London, a somewhat coarser version of Em's own accent that had been softened by her three years at RADA.

They only stayed for a little over an hour, just long enough for Kay to be introduced and for them all to drink a cup of tea. Seeing a fellow male in the house, Jim immediately jumped to the conclusion that Kay would be interested in anything car related and proceeded to regale him with tales of Holley carbs, high-lift camshafts and final-drive ratios. In fact, Kay had little interest in cars other than as a method of getting from A to B and virtually everything Jim said flew high above his head but still, he couldn't help liking the big West Indian.

After a few minutes Pat loudly intervened, 'Stop boring him with all that stuff. I doubt if he's got any interest in cars, have you Kay?'

'Well um…' began Kay realising he had two choices, firstly to admit his lack of any interest whatever in the subject and risk offending Jim, or secondly, pretend that he was avidly absorbing the string of meaningless words and phrases that kept being tossed his way, the downside of which was that he would potentially have to endure a rather tedious three-quarters of an hour. Kay, of course chose the latter.

'No ,it's fine,' he replied, not sure whether to add 'Patience,' 'it's fine, I like cars'.

Jim however had picked up the vibe and, much to Kay's relief, said in his strong Jamaican accent, 'no she's right, I am going on a bit. What would you like, football or religion?'

'Don't you dare,' interjected Patience, 'you've known the man five minutes and you want to pick his religion to bits. Just stick to football!'.

Out of the corner of his eye, Kay could just see Em laughing to herself.

*

'You really look like your Mum,' said Kay during the short drive home.

'I hope I do. She was gorgeous when she was younger'.

'She's not so bad now,' Kay added, not too sure whether it was the right thing to say.

'So, you fancy my Mum?' said Em with mock indignation.

'Now did I say that?' Kay retorted, taking her much too seriously. 'I just meant she was er… very good for her age. Besides I'd have Big Jim to cope with'.

'So how old do you think she is? Fifty? Fifty Five? No, she's forty two. She was just eighteen when Ethel was born'.

'And what happened to your father?' said Kay shifting the subject slightly. He really had found Patience quite attractive and an appealing if unfortunate image had come into his mind of indulging in a ménage à trois with mother and daughter, an image which was proving very hard to dispel.

'He got killed,' said Em. 'A disagreement with a guy in South London somewhere. The dude pulled out a knife and stabbed him through the heart. The papers described it as a gangland murder. I don't like to think about him too much and Mum never mentions him either. After that Mum had a series of abusive boyfriends,' Em continued, 'One of them actually did time for bashing her about. She often had black eyes when I was a kid. Jim has been good for her though but she does grit her teeth when it comes to the cars.'

Kay had noticed that her slight London accent strengthened to almost true Cockney levels when she was talking with her family and it was now clear that this trait extended to discussions merely concerning them. It was as if she had to think herself back into a part she was now reprising after many years performing other roles. Far from thinking this strange, he actually found it quite endearing, a new facet to her personality that he had not noticed before.

Chapter Ten

Monday July 19th 2010

Of course, a reciprocal arrangement had to be made and as Monday was the only day Em was guaranteed to get off, it had to be the following Monday straight after work. Kay had a business meeting in Horsham that day and was able to get back early enough to avoid the worst of the traffic. Ruth had insisted that they come over for dinner and had quizzed Kay in great detail about Em's likes and dislikes, to which he replied 'anything in moderation'.

Kay couldn't help but notice that Em was on edge during the journey to Amersham. She wasn't her usual sunny self and when Kay asked her what the problem was, she sighed, 'Oh, I don't know. Our backgrounds are so far apart, I'm not sure I'll know how to behave. They're sure to think I'm common'.

'You do talk some bollocks, just be yourself and they'll love you'.

'Promise?'

'Of course. They're not royalty. My Dad's Dad was a coal miner and my Mum's Mum worked in Woolworth's. 'So...,' Kay continued firmly, 'so it's a first night, your make-up has been done, you know all your lines, and you're ready to meet your audience. You hear your cue and step out onto the stage. At that point you don't say to yourself, 'I don't think I can do this,' you just get out there and give it your all. After a few seconds you know you're winning. Yes?'.

'Yes'. She smiled, put her hand on his knee, and despite the constraints of the seatbelt, leaned over and nuzzled his shoulder.

*

Ruth opened the door and immediately embraced Kay as was her wont. 'Hello Kenny love,' she said with a broad smile on her face, 'and who's this?' She did, of course, know who it was as Kay had already told her, but mother and son kept up the pretence in order to welcome Em as a probationary member of their family.

'Hello Mum, this is Em'.

'Hi,' said Em, not entirely sure how to address Ruth.

'Just call me Ruth,' she said anticipating the question.

Kay had told his parents nothing about Em other than that she was his new girlfriend and that they had moved into a flat together in Shepherd's Bush. It was therefore up to them to find out whatever they could. Some things were obvious, she was not very tall, had coffee coloured skin, a figure that most women would envy (and men covet) and a beautiful smile.

In fact, other than her height she was the perfect physical specimen that most parents would wish to see their son bring home.

Em looked around her, 'What a lovely house'.

'We like it,' smiled Richard in response.

'Em has an interesting job,' said Kay knowing that this was one conversation she would never want to start. He knew from experience that she would try to play down, or not even mention her occupation as it tended to make her the queen bee, something she always desperately, but usually ineffectively, tried to avoid. Nonetheless his parents would love to know.

'Okay, so spill the beans Em,' said Richard in his friendliest tone, 'are you a brain surgeon, an astronaut, a deep-sea diver…?'

'No, nothing like that, ' laughed Em, 'I'm an actor'.

'Gosh,' said Ruth open-mouthed, 'Will we have seen you in anything?'

'I doubt it, I've rarely been in anything much on telly, other than the odd advert'.

'Do you know the Sunray Shampoo advert?' interjected Kay.

'I think so,' said Richard.

Kay simply made a hand gesture towards Em who pretended to take a bow.

It was a lovely July evening and the four of them sat in the garden drinking whatever took their fancy while Jack wandered back and forth between the house and the garden, a glass of Coke in one hand and a Nintendo DSi in the other. Setting these down on the grass, he found a football in a flower bed and crashed it as hard as he could into the net which was positioned at the end of the lawn. *'Goooooooaaaaaal!'* he shouted at the top of his voice.

Kay was half inclined to get up and join him in an impromptu game, but he felt he couldn't leave Em as she had only just been introduced to his parents. To be fair though, she was more than holding her own, answering questions about her career and the famous actors she'd met. Despite them both having full-time jobs, the Nettletons stuck to the traditional model of wife cooking, husband clearing up afterwards which meant that after a while Ruth re-located herself to the kitchen, leaving their guest to the two men.

Richard, it seemed was entirely captivated by the beautiful young woman his elder son had brought to meet them and chatted to her at every possible opportunity.

Jack continued to play football noisily against an imaginary opposition while the adults talked among themselves. After a while, the ball rolled towards Em who got out of her chair and chipped the ball accurately back to Jack who turned and headed the ball into the goal.

'You didn't tell me you could play football,' exclaimed Kay.

'You never asked. I used to play for my school girls' team – striker, fox in the box, that was me. In my last year at school I scored twenty one goals'.

'Is there anything you're not good at?'

Em thought for a moment, 'Insurance'.

Just then Ruth called them in for dinner. Richard and Em went in first while Kay accompanied his younger brother. With a perception that belied his years, Jack looked at Kay and said, 'Punching above your weight there aren't you bro?'

Kay turned round, picked Jack up and threw him over his shoulder.

'Aaggh, put me down!' shouted Jack. Kay dropped him abruptly.

'Ow, you sod,' complained Jack loudly taking a swipe at Kay's back.

'Jack, no swearing please,' came Ruth's voice from the kitchen, 'we've got a guest'.

Kay entered the house thinking about Jack's jibe. Perhaps he really was punching above his weight. Perhaps most men would feel that way with a woman as beautiful as Em. He only had to watch their faces as he walked down the street with her. She was a real head turner.

Dinner was a simple meal of grilled salmon, new potatoes and vegetables followed by a fresh fruit salad. Em took her usual diminutive portions and any surplus was polished off by Jack who seemed to be capable of eating whatever sized meal was put in front of him in double-quick time and then helping himself to more.

Having by some distance the most interesting job of anyone round the table, it was not surprising that much of the conversation was directed towards Em. She was, however, used to this and followed a tactic that Kay had noticed before, of attempting to deflect the discussion in other directions. As a result, the conversation flitted from one topic to another finally settling, no one was quite sure how, on the environment.

'Kenny's always been interested in nature,' smiled Ruth.

'I know,' replied Em with a smile, 'I've been dragged off for lots of country walks over the last couple of months. He's tried to teach me the names of all the birds. I'm learning, slowly. But I still can't tell a sparrow from a dunnock!'

'… Or a woodpecker from a lesser spotted tit warbler,' interjected Kay.

'Now you're taking the mickey out of me. I can't help being a city girl'.

Kay's first impulse was to make a joke on the subject of great tits but the presence of his parents prevented him from doing so. He would have to remember it and use it on some future occasion. Instead, he just laughed in what he hoped was a kindly fashion.

Nevertheless, Em still scowled and kicked him under the table.

*

It was dark by the time they left Amersham. There were very few vehicles about and the most exciting thing on the road was the constant stream of cat's eyes as, one by one, they vanished from view somewhere to the car's right.

'You were brilliant tonight, 'They loved you and you had my Dad eating out of your hand'.

'They were nicer than I'd expected. Your Dad's a sweetie and your Mum was nice too'. She paused. 'There's been something I've been meaning to say to you and what we were talking about tonight just made me think about it even more'.

'Okay, fire away.'

'I still find it hard to understand why you stick in insurance when you hate it so much,' she sighed, '… and I know it's easy for me because I love what I do. But have you ever thought of getting a job where you're working in the countryside?'

'Jack it all in, just like that?' replied Kay, 'Well, two big reasons. Firstly, the money. I get paid well at G & B, far more than I'm worth and far more than I'd get up country. More importantly though, what would happen to us? You're completely tied to London and working as a wildlife warden or whatever will mean me being based Christ knows where, but almost certainly nowhere near London. And I'd need qualifications'.

'I could just stop applying for stage work and concentrate on film, television and adverts,' countered Em, 'Filming can take place anywhere and where I lived wouldn't matter'.

'It's a thought,' mused Kay, but something inside him was saying that whatever he did would bite into Em's prospects. Although she had done well for her age, she still wasn't established in what he knew could be a highly precarious occupation. Em's happiness was crucial to him and he felt she would be giving up too much.

Em however read his mind. 'Please don't think of me, it's you who's important here and it winds me up to see you in such a rut'.

In truth, this was something that Kay had been thinking about for years but he kept up a parody of the defence for a little longer. 'Ah the joys of insurance' he said with mock wistfulness, 'the sheer pleasure of inspecting a rubber factory in Droitwich, the thrill of filling in a proposal for a pig farm near Slough or the ecstasy of investigating a claim for damage to a Portaloo in Chipping Sodbury... Yes, it's a wonderful life in commercial insurance'.

Em sighed. 'I love you as you are, but sometimes you really piss me off. There are times when I wish you'd take things more seriously. You hide behind this *façade* of humour just so as you can avoid taking a decision. You've got to get out of it. It's shit and you know it'.

'You're right.' Kay replied in a more serious tone, 'There are actually rumours going the rounds that Tony wants to sell up. If I hold on for a bit longer, I might be able to wangle some redundancy money out of it'.

Chapter Eleven

Summer – Autumn 2010

Whenever people consider working-class London, most will immediately think of the East End, 'Knees Up Mother Brown', cockney rhyming slang, pearly kings and queens but the west side of London has always had a thriving working-class culture too. Where the East End had waves of immigrants, most notably Huguenots, Ashkenazy Jews and more recently Bangladeshis, the West had the Irish.

Despite the fact that there were now people of many nations living in Shepherd's Bush and the part of West London within the North Circular Road, there was still a background of Irishness about the place. Had she known it, this was the community from which Em's late father came. The Irish diaspora of West London have included newsworthy individuals from all walks of life but the acting profession, for some reason, stands out. From their ranks have emerged such notables as Joss Ackland, Susan Hampshire, Alan Rickman and Daniel Radcliffe.

Although much of their road had now been gentrified, Kay found that 'The Bush' generally had an attractive edginess about it and, unlike his erstwhile home in Chorleywood, it was possible to get virtually anything you could need at any time of the day or night.

*

Em left her role at The Globe in the middle of August and following a brief holiday in Gran Canaria, the two of them spent much of their time either at home or in one or other of the pubs or bars in the locality. Em's days were occasionally punctuated by auditions but other than one advert, this time for a breakfast cereal, she had thus far been unsuccessful.

On his way home one day Kay received a text from Em asking him to pick her up from her mother's house. This was not unusual and Kay did not mind in the least. He had become quite friendly with Jim even if he did sometimes have to steer him gently away from the subject of cars.

It was one of those grey late summer days when rain never seemed that far away and the windscreen wipers were permanently on intermittent wipe. He parked the old Escort some three houses along from Pat and Jim's place, checked his phone, got out and locked the door. Out of the corner of his eye he caught a movement in the hedge. The movement was followed by a heavy thud at the back of his head and everything went black.

*

The next thing he remembered was slowly coming round in an ambulance with Em sitting beside him holding his hand and looking panic-stricken.

'Oh, thank God,' she said in a shaky voice.

Kay tried to reply but his mouth was dry and the pain in his head was excruciating.

'Just lie still,' said a kindly female voice from somewhere behind his head, 'we'll soon be there'.

Kay looked around at all the medical paraphernalia of a modern ambulance but was unable to take in any detail. He could scarcely see the paramedic between him and the front of the ambulance, but got the impression of a calm, steadying presence. 'Nearly there…' she intoned.

The hospital was little more than half a mile from Mellitus Street but by the time they got there, Kay had recovered most of his faculties. It was just the pain in his head that still troubled him.

He was wheeled out of the ambulance, down a corridor and into a small, curtained bay in the Accident and Emergency Department. Em had followed the trolley and was now sitting on a chair beside him. As soon as the porter had left, Kay turned to her and said, 'Well, what happened?'

'Ryan happened,' she almost spat out the words, and then more softly, 'it's a long story'.

'Well it looks like I'm going to have a fair bit of time on my hands so you might as well tell me.'

She looked at him, touched his cheek and started, 'So, before I met you I briefly dated this guy called Ryan – Ryan Browne. He was okay at first, very attentive but things rapidly went downhill.

Attentive became obsessive and I just couldn't go anywhere without his turning up. I told him to clear off, like 'it's over' but he wouldn't take no for an answer. In the end I reported him to the police who hauled him in and gave him a warning. But it didn't do any good'.

'I think something's falling into place,' Kay exclaimed. 'Was he the guy outside The Dove on our first date?'

'Yep, that was him. He'd obviously followed me all the way from Shepherd's Bush. It was no accident that he was there. After a while I stopped seeing him around and I thought he'd got the message, but then over the last two or three weeks I was sure I'd seen him hanging about near our flat'.

'So why didn't you tell me?'

'I don't know, I wish I had now so you'd have been on your guard but… Oh God, I wish I had. It was kind of embarrassing I suppose. Nobody likes to admit they've got a stalker'.

'And so what happened to him?'

'Fortunately, Mum's next door neighbour saw everything. Jim rushed out and between the two of them they managed to catch him. We phoned the police who took twenty minutes to arrive. Jim wasn't all that gentle, so Ryan was in a bit of a mess by the time they turned up. You seriously wouldn't want to get on the wrong side of Jim. Fortunately one of the two policemen had had previous experience of Ryan. He just winked at Jim, put Ryan in handcuffs and stuffed him roughly in the back of the car. ' She paused for a second or two, 'I was really worried about you, you just didn't move'. Tears ran down her cheeks. 'I don't think I could have lived with myself if you'd been seriously hurt'.

It was now Kay's turn to offer a consoling word, 'It wasn't your fault. How could you possibly be to blame for some nutter who has taken a shine to you? Given that this is common assault, I doubt if we'll see this Ryan Browne character for some time'.

The hospital kept Kay in overnight for observation but they were satisfied he had nothing more than concussion and discharged him the following morning. Jim had found the weapon – a block of wood that the assailant had probably found on a building site across the road. To that extent the attack was not pre-meditated but it didn't help Kay feel any more charitable towards the culprit. 'They should lock the bastard up and throw away the key,' he said before realising that give or take a Yorkshire accent he was sounding exactly like his late paternal grandfather.

Chapter Twelve

It was autumn and the general pattern of their lives was now set. Unless he had a meeting at a client's premises, Kay would leave the flat at seven thirty for his office in the city, returning between six thirty and seven o'clock in the evening. Em was working lunchtimes and occasional evenings in the Princess Victoria, a pub just a short walk along the Uxbridge Road in the direction of Acton. Occasionally she would have to take time off to attend auditions but was almost always unsuccessful.

One evening Kay returned to find Em staring with a vacant expression at *The One Show*, a programme she seldom, if ever, watched. That morning she'd been to an audition for a new three episode mini-series ITV were making, due to be filmed over the winter in London and on location in Devon. She'd told Kay that her chances of landing anything were minimal, but it was her lot as an actor to keep on trying. There might just be the chance of a very minor role if she played her cards right.

Kay was used to Em's downcast moods following an unsuccessful audition and usually he would pussy-foot around the subject hoping that she would tell him, unprompted, that once again she hadn't got the part. This procedure usually took the whole of the evening to play out. He didn't know why but, on this occasion, he launched straight in with a cheery, 'So how did it go then?'

Em looked up from *The One Show*, stretched, got off the sofa and then announced as if to a large audience, 'They like me! They've got me on hold. That means I can't apply for anything else until next Friday - not that I was going to anyway. They'll probably want to see me again around the middle of next week.'

'That's fantastic,' said Kay, 'so I guess it's just a case of keeping our fingers crossed. You can do it Em, I know you can!'.

After a second or two, Em turned to Kay and said softly, 'You know, I have a good feeling about this. The casting director was a really nice guy and he seemed to take to me. It could be my big breakthrough!'

Kay looked her in the eye. 'You deserve it,' he said, 'all those times you've got up early in the morning for fruitless auditions only to be rejected after a few seconds. It's got to wear you down after a while'.

Em now looked Kay directly in the eye, 'I've never asked you this before but do you mind what I do? Okay, let me rephrase that, does it worry you that I'm an actress?' Unusually she had used the feminine form of the noun. On most occasions she used the androgynous 'actor'.

'Well I can't say that I would be overfond of you doing porn movies, but I've never known you as anything else, other than a barmaid but that's just filling in time. Look, although we're a couple we still have our own lives to lead. I don't believe you should interfere with a person's very essence, what makes them

79

tick - because, apart from anything else, that could destroy whatever attracted you to them in the first place.'

'Doesn't it worry you that relationships with actors can be well... short'.

'Yes, of course it does,' replied Kay, 'but I can't do anything about it. How can I influence the fact that actress x has been married ten times and had umpteen affaires? I just have to trust to luck and treat you right'. Returning his gaze, she whispered 'Nobody has ever treated me better'. She kissed him and they sat silently together for twenty minutes or more, neither of them wanting to break the spell.

Eventually Kay whispered softly, 'I think it's my turn to cook dinner'. He rose from the sofa and, given the potential importance of the occasion, began to prepare one of his trademark chicken curries.

*

Kay had been speaking from the heart when he said that he was afraid of losing her if her career took off. But what could he do? He couldn't keep her like a bird in a gilded cage as (he assumed) Ryan had tried to do. Although they actually had very little in common, he loved this girl and was going to try his damndest to keep hold of her. But barely a day went by without the tabloid press reporting that this famous actor or that famous actress had split with their partner and gone off with somebody else they had met on set, so he knew that there was the potential for a worrying future ahead of him.

The studio rang Em the following Tuesday and she immediately called Kay to tell him that they wanted her to come in for a further screen test the next day. His heart began to pound. Despite his concerns about the threat to their relationship, he was really rooting for her. He wanted her to get the part unconditionally because he knew it was what she had always wanted.

Kay went to work as normal on Wednesday. His colleagues in the office were now used to the fact that his partner was a budding actress. As she hadn't appeared in anything more exciting than the muesli advert which went out the previous month, interest was beginning to wane and she was now just the 'normal' girlfriend of a work colleague.

At three thirty Kay's mobile pinged. It was a text from Em and it said simply, '*I got the part!!*'.

Kay let out a muted, 'Yes!' and leaned back in his seat. Intrigued, Raj came over to his desk, 'What's happened? Won the lottery? Tony fallen off a cliff?'

'Neither of those things, welcome though they'd be. Em has just landed a big part in a TV show.' 'Great! 'What's it called? When's it going out?'

'No idea. F.A.I.D.C. as Mike would say'.

In fact, the mini-series was called, '*The Broken Pane*'. It concerned a young woman whose brother had been murdered. The plot revolved around her attempts to find the culprit and the relationship between her and the world-weary private investigator she hires to help solve the mystery. It had been written by a reasonably well-known scriptwriter and was expected to do well.

On his way home that evening, Kay dropped in to a little shop he knew just off the Tottenham Court Road and bought a bottle of vintage champagne to share with Em that evening. Unsurprisingly, when he arrived he found her in a high state of euphoria and unable to remain still for more than a couple of seconds at a time.

Forgetting the champagne, Kay shook his head and said, 'Look, why don't we go out for a meal tonight and perhaps that'll stop you jumping up and down like a jack-in-the-box'.

Finding most of their usual haunts fully booked, they eventually got a table at a little Indian restaurant in Turnham Green. In addition to her acting talents, Em possessed a pretty decent voice in the soprano register which had been honed at RADA, and all the way to the restaurant she sang a medley of songs from artists as diverse as The Spice Girls, Beyoncé and Ella Fitzgerald at something approaching the top of her voice. By the time they got there and found somewhere to park, Kay's ears were ringing.

'Jesus wept! I feel like I've just been in a cross between grand opera and a rock concert,' he said again shaking his head and twisting his finger in his right ear as if trying to expel the sound.

'I'm just so happy. It's what I've always dreamed of,' replied Em with a laugh. 'You're not going to be a sourpuss tonight of all nights are you?'

'Would I do that?' he said pulling her close to him. They kissed and walked into the restaurant.

For the first half hour, Em chatted away more or less continuously, but as the evening wore on she became more and more reserved.

'It's just beginning to sink in,' she said softly, 'it could all go horribly wrong. What if I'm rubbish, what if they change their minds?'

'First of all, you couldn't be rubbish even if you tried your hardest. Don't forget I *have* seen you act and you were brilliant. Secondly, why on Earth would they change their minds? This is what you've trained hard for. It's your big opportunity. Once the adrenalin starts flowing you'll be able to take it in your stride. Believe me'.

Em toyed absentmindedly with the wine glass in front of her. 'I suppose you're right but it all seems so daunting now'.

Despite his assurances however, her mood remained low-key for the rest of the evening and the bottle of champagne remained untouched.

Chapter Thirteen

October – December 2010

In addition to his understandable interest in the pending upturn in Em's career, Kay was constantly turning over in his mind her suggestion that he change career in order to earn a living doing something in which he had more interest. There was a paradox in his thinking here. He had put a huge amount of effort into his attempts to date Em but when it came to choosing jobs he had just followed the line of least resistance. Yes, he had changed employer twice but in both cases, his new employer had pursued him as much as he had pursued them. In any event, her suggestion had left him in limbo. He had less and less interest in his work but rumours concerning the possible sale of G & B persisted. If he left now he could forego a substantial redundancy package which, in itself, could smooth his passage into a new occupation. In the meantime therefore, he felt he had no choice but to soldier on.

Kay was not the only one in the office to feel this way. Both Jayne and Raj were unsettled and like him, waiting for the outcome of any negotiations. The interested party was reported to be Levison Drake plc, a large insurance broker that covered everything from pensions and investments to large scale marine underwriting. In the last ten years they had scoured the country for small brokerage firms to add to their portfolio. Their usual *modus operandi* was to buy the firm, make most of the staff redundant and move operations to their head office in Bristol. Their sole interest was the client base and in the fullness of time even the name of the acquisition would disappear.

Although harsh, this would suit many of G & B's disaffected staff. As they were the ones with day to day contact with the clients, the middle rank which included Kay, Jayne and Raj were the least likely to be affected. Levison Drake and their ilk knew that if you removed the person who actually knew the customer, saw them face to face and shared the odd beer with them, they could easily set up on their own and take their customer bank with them. Hence, if they were made redundant they would in all probability benefit from enhanced terms but would have to agree not to poach their erstwhile clients for a certain period of time.

*

Gresham & Bailey was an old-fashioned firm in the sense that there were no self-contained workstations which would have turned each worker into the clerical equivalent of a battery hen, hermetically sealed from his or her co-workers. Despite bucking the trend to the undoubted benefit of his staff, this was not due to any paternalistic feelings for their mental welfare on Tony Bailey's part, merely that he was convinced that it would be expensive to re-arrange the workspace and the plug sockets on which the office relied. Nobody that worked there was about to tell him otherwise. As a result the offices of G & B were laid out in an open-plan configuration, exactly as they had always been.

This meant that there was a constant flow of conversation between members of staff. The concept of the discussion around the water-cooler was entirely redundant and not only for the fact that G & B did not possess a water cooler. Good-natured ribbing, quips of varying descriptions as well as the odd practical joke tended to be the rule. The unwary could find rubber bands in their sandwiches or they may arrive home unwittingly displaying an office coat hanger on their belt or have a six foot chain of paperclips attached to the hem of their coat. All good undergraduate stuff which the po-faced denizens of commerce have in recent years sought to extinguish from our national business life with a good deal of success, more's the pity.

A fair amount of serious stuff got discussed too. There would often be heated political discussions which Mike tried, usually unsuccessfully, to damp down.

The news of Em's major role in *The Broken Pane* had become a hot topic of conversation. It had not taken long for Raj to be persuaded to let the cat out of the bag and once it was out, everybody wanted to pump Kay on the subject. When was it being shot? When was it going to be shown? Who else was going to be in it? and even, 'can I have her autograph for my daughter?' On this final point Kay was happy to oblige and unsurprisingly Em was thoroughly flattered.

*

Shooting was due to start at the end of November. Kay was every bit as keyed up as Em but the noticeably short Autumn days and correspondingly long nights were beginning to drag. She was increasingly absorbed in reading the script and learning her lines. He helped out by acting as a dummy audience whenever she required but understandably her preparations meant that they had to stay in most nights. His consolation was simply how happy it made her. The crisis of confidence she had shown that night had long disappeared and she was going at her task with gusto. Kay was reminded of the night at the National Theatre when, even though he was no expert, it was clear to him that she was potentially a very good actor indeed.

At eight a.m. on Monday 29 November, Em left the flat for her first day of filming on the South Bank, not returning, completely drained, until gone nine that evening. This routine continued right up until a couple of days before Christmas with Kay acting as chief cook and general housekeeper, running baths and making sure that she was refreshed for the next day.

As most couples do, they divided Christmas between their two sets of parents, Christmas Day being spent at Pat and Jim's little place which was crowded fit to burst with the four of them, Ethel (whom Kay had already discovered, was called Sassie by the family), her partner Dave, their daughter Ruby and Jim's twelve year old son Marvin who was already head and shoulders above Em.

This was the first time Kay had met Sassie and he found her completely different to her sister. She had curly rather than straight hair, was a little taller and plumper than Em with a slightly harsh voice that betrayed the location of her birth. She was good company though, with a sardonic sense of humour. Her childhood ambition had always been to enter the teaching profession but finding herself pregnant at the age of seventeen, she had had to accept that this would not happen any time soon. To tide her over, in what she considered to be a temporary halfway house, she worked as a teaching assistant in a primary school in Oxhey.

Despite their obvious differences, from such things as the way they finished each other's sentences, it was clear to Kay that the sisters were actually very close.

'So what was she like as a kid?' Kay asked Sassie while the remains of the turkey were still sitting abandoned on the table.

'Don't you dare!' interjected Em.

'Ha!' replied Sassie completely ignoring her, 'she was a little prima donna. Always pestering Mum to take her to ballet classes, singing lessons or anything really. I tell you what was irritating though, she was always so good at whatever she did. Don't people like that really annoy you?' she laughed.

'You went to ballet too,' objected Em

'Only for a few weeks,' her sister replied. 'to be fair though, you were way better than me,' and turning to Kay, 'athletics was my thing. I represented London Schools at two hundred and four hundred metres. I could have been an Olympic athlete but then things happened…'. She looked across at Ruby, by now fast asleep on Dave's lap.

Pat joined the conversation, 'The amount of overtime I worked to pay for those ballet lessons…'.

This direct connection between earning and spending was unfamiliar to Kay from his elevated position on the top half of the social ladder. Economic theory had taught him about the propensity of people on lower incomes to immediately spend a high proportion of any additional income they received. This would not have been the case for people in his parents' position. He had, of course, experienced it for himself as a student but he always knew that his parents would support him if things went wrong. Pat however would have had no safety net to rely on other than the faceless bureaucracy of the State. For Kay this served to throw the differences in their family backgrounds into even sharper relief.

Jim and Pat were in many ways simple folk but he always looked forward to seeing them and the day passed quickly, watching television and playing board games as well as drinking large quantities of Stella Artois, Vodka Martinis and a completely random selection of other alcoholic drinks.

The drinking and driving laws dictated that driving home was out of the question although Kay and Em could just about have walked to their flat had they so wished. Fortunately, there was just about enough room at the house for everyone to at least grab a reasonable size patch of floor to crash down for the night. Kay and Em settled for the living room with Kay ceding the sofa to Em while he spent an uncomfortable night on the floor listening to the tick of a rather noisy clock.

They had planned to spend Boxing Day with Kay's parents but their plans were put on hold when, far from responding to the ignition key, the old Escort just made a loud click. Jim was of course on hand to help but Kay felt bad about asking for his assistance on what was a cold and drizzly morning. After a minute or two Jim diagnosed a failed starter solenoid. He immediately went out to the back garden, grubbed around in his shed for another couple of minutes, found a replacement, fitted it and ten minutes later they were on the road.

The highlight of their day in Amersham was the family kick about after lunch. The garden was deemed too small for this activity and so despite the failing daylight they went to a local park for what had, over the years ,become a ritual in the Nettleton family. With one extra player this year, they could actually have a competitive game, Jack and his father against Kay and Em. Despite complaining that Kay was constantly fouling him, Jack and Richard emerged the victors by the score of seven goals to four. This was very much not Ruth's scene and she remained firmly indoors during the whole of the proceedings, relaxing after the stresses of preparing the Boxing Day meal.

Again Kay and Em stayed the night, somewhat earlier to bed and in rather more comfort than the previous night. As Christmas and Boxing Day had been on Saturday and Sunday that year, there was no great rush to head off the following day. Em however, had to get back to filming on the twenty ninth and needed time to prepare, so they headed back to Shepherd's Bush mid-afternoon.

'I like your family,' smiled Em as they approached the Hanger Lane Gyratory System, 'but their way of life is just so different from mine. I'd never been to a house and a garden that big before I met you. All my friends' parents rented - I'm obviously the girl from the wrong side of the tracks'.

Kay was not sure how seriously to take this but after some consideration, said in reply, 'When you're a big star, you'll have half a dozen houses twice as big as my Mum and Dad's'.

'Fat chance,' sighed Em.

Chapter Fourteen

Filming at the studio ended on 21 January. There was then a week's gap before the centre of operations moved to Devon. This would be the first time for many months that Kay and Em would be separated for more than the odd day. Although he was no stranger to living by himself, Kay was not looking forward to the two weeks Em would be away and not just because he would miss her. As his perceptive little brother had indicated, he was all too afraid he was 'punching above his weight' and filming on location would provide plenty of opportunities for Em to stray from the straight and narrow. He knew how he would behave if he was a young actor spending two weeks in a hotel with a woman as beautiful as Em and that worried him.

The two weeks passed surprisingly quickly with an immense amount of texting traffic between them. Kay learnt that the leading man had appeared in many television programmes and full-length feature films. For a while, he had decamped to Hollywood but things did not really work out for him there and he returned eighteen months later. He was all right, Em confided but a little full of himself for her taste. Much of the filming took place on Aylesbeare Common which according to Em was absolutely freezing at that time of year.

For his part, Kay went drinking after work for four of the ten nights in the company of various work colleagues. To make up for the damage this would wreak on his waistline, another two nights saw him visit a gym for extended workouts. He had recently joined a local football club and turned out for them at North Acton Playing Fields on the Sunday. He much preferred playing here among the terraced and semi-detached houses of inter-war suburbia than on the bleak and windswept Wormwood Scrubs. As it happened, he surprised everyone, including himself, by scoring the second goal in a 3-2 victory and spent much of the day socialising with his new team mates.

Em was due to return on Saturday February 12th and, not knowing how she would be feeling, he decided to cook her a meal rather than eat out. The vintage champagne he had bought in the autumn still lay unopened in the fridge and he earmarked it to be drunk that night. As she was still unable to drive, she had taken the train from Waterloo to Honiton and her return journey would be a reverse of this.

Kay caught the underground from Shepherd's Bush Market in plenty of time to meet her train. He would have driven but the thought of driving a significant distance in Inner London filled him with dread. So the old Escort remained somewhat less than perfectly parked in Coverdale Road.

He knew her train would be delayed as she had texted to tell him but it crawled through the London suburbs and when it finally pulled in at 19.05, it was thirty seven minutes overdue. Em was not the easiest person to see amongst the throng of disgruntled passengers disgorged onto Platform 11 but he eventually spotted her, wearing a full length coat that he recognised and a scarf that he did not.

Smiling, she approached him and immediately threw her arms around his neck.

'I've missed you,' she whispered in his ear.

'Really?' he replied, 'with all those hunks straight out of acting school?'.

She took one step back and poked her tongue out at him. He laughed and they fell back towards each other again. If she had strayed while she was away, she was not showing any sign of it.

'Come on, we don't want to spend all day here. Dinner will be late enough as it is.'

Em talked almost incessantly on the way home about the well-known people she had met both on the acting and the production side of the industry,

'… and then there was Jamie, the Head of Photography. He's worked on some of the Star Wars films…'.

'So who was Boom Operator then?'

'Oh, that was Martin. Why do you ask?'.

'Well every television production seems to have a boom operator and I haven't the foggiest idea what he does.'

She tutted, 'So he's the guy that operates the boom. Don't you know anything?'

The Bakerloo Line train rattled to a halt at Paddington. They got out and walked briskly through the tunnels and up the escalator to the Hammersmith & City Line platforms. After a five minute wait they caught the train which ran largely above ground to Shepherd's Bush Market station. This can seem to be a very slow section of track along which the train ambles sclerotically, stopping at Royal Oak, Westbourne Park, Ladbroke Grove, Latimer Road, the new station at Wood Lane and eventually what has since 2008 been called Shepherd's Bush Market Station. This was unfortunate as they were both in something of a hurry...

When the train finally disgorged them into the night air, they almost ran back to the flat and both of them knew why.

Kay did not have a bad memory but he desperately needed reminding of the attractions of Em's naked body. Of course, nothing about her had changed and they spent the next hour making love.

Eventually their appetite for sex waned as their need for food grew and they finally sat down to dinner at a shade before ten o'clock. Whilst she was not looking, Kay took the bottle of champagne from the fridge and covered it with a clean tea towel. As they were about to eat, he stood up, whisked off the tea towel and removed the cork with a loud 'pop'!

'Here's to the new Greta Garbo,' said Kay bowing in the manner of a dutiful servant.

'Not Greta Garbo please. She wanted to be alone. Hardly me is it?'

'Well then, Angelina Jolie, Cate Blanchett, Emma Stone...'.

'I don't want to be the new anybody,' Em interrupted, 'Just the first me'.

'Okay, here's to the one and only...' Kay imitated a fanfare of trumpets, '...Emma Silvester. God bless her and all who sail in her'.

'Clown!' laughed Em.

He poured the champagne and they clinked glasses.

'And here's to the world's greatest insurance broker, although he really should be doing something else…' countered Em.

*

The following day, Kay was due to play football at a particularly wet and windy Pitch 14 on Wormwood Scrubs. He had played there before and hated it. As well as being anonymous and sloping, the pitches were often littered with all sorts of detritus – dog excreta, dead hedgehogs, used condoms… Much against his better judgement, he asked Em to come along and for the first time, watch him play. Not to put too fine a point on it, he had a stinker. Mid-way through the second half he under hit a pass back to his goalkeeper. The ball stuck in the West London mud and the opposition left winger who had been getting on his nerves all afternoon, nipped in and put the ball in the net. To make matters worse he jeered at Kay on his way back to the halfway line for the restart. It was as much as he could do to stop himself from thumping the irritating little man - he probably would have done if Em had not been there.

The game finished 1-0 and after the final whistle, he went over to her on the touchline.

'That was fucking shit'. Kay seldom swore in Em's presence and it startled her.

'I'm sorry,' he continued, noticing the effect his bad temper had had. 'Not my best game today I'm afraid'.

'Don't worry,' Em replied having regained her composure, 'I think that little twat would have wound me up too,' she nodded in the direction of the

opposition goalscorer, now swaggering off the pitch with an insufferable smirk on his face.

He left her to the mercy of the other wives and girlfriends and started the long walk back to the changing rooms.

'Sorry lads,' Kay said to the other team members also heading for a well-deserved shower.

'Don't worry, it happens,' replied Ed Mayo, a man now in his early forties and for as long as anybody could remember, team captain of Acton Athletic F.C.

'Ere,' Brandon Ward, one of the team's younger players exclaimed, alternating his glance between Kay and Em whose form was now disappearing among a throng of wet and miserable spectators slowly trooping away from the pitch, 'you're a bit of a dark 'orse. I wouldn't mind one of those myself, 'as she got a sister?'

Despite the overt sexism in the comment, its effect was to slightly raise the cloud above Kay's head. He didn't mind other men envying him for his beautiful girlfriend and the comment helped dispel his frustration at what he saw as his poor performance on the pitch.

'She has but spoken for I'm afraid,' replied Kay with the ghost of a smile.

'Shame,' retorted Brandon.

Chapter Fifteen

The wait for ITV to announce the dates on which _The Broken Pane_ was to be screened became unbearable for both Em and Kay. To counter their complete inability to relax, it was agreed between them that they had to get away for a while. As a result, Kay booked a week's holiday in Malta for the two of them. But just before they were about to leave, Em received an email telling her that the series of three programmes were to be broadcast from Monday the 16th to Wednesday the 18th of May.

Although this allayed the (very unlikely) concern that the production was too dire to broadcast, the holiday was now all the more necessary to take their minds off of how it would be received. It was not quite make or break for Em's career but if the series bombed and her performance took a panning from the critics, then she would be back to adverts and understudy roles for the foreseeable future.

So, on the 16th of April they caught a plane from Stanstead Airport to Valletta. There is something about a holiday location before the season really kicks off. The sun is not as hot, the winds are keener and the whole place has the atmosphere of a theatre playing host to the dress rehearsal of some great play.

Without a surplus of humanity, it is possible to see the bones of the place, the things that make it tick, the shuttered bars yet to open, the screws that hold up the empty shelves in the souvenir shops.

Nonetheless, there was enough to make their holiday well worthwhile despite the necessity to sit inside the taverns for their evening meal. Although there was the odd rain shower, the winds were light and the temperature was mostly in the high teens or early twenties and they both managed to simply lie out in the sun, if only for short periods.

Because they were both waiting for something dramatic to happen in their working lives, Em far more than Kay, the holiday had an unusual feel. They still made love as frequently and energetically as before but it was obvious to Kay that the immediate future was hanging heavily on Em's mind. Although she was happy to discuss other matters, *The Broken Pane* and even its potential consequences were strictly off limits.

'So when you're a big star we'll be able to take a dozen holidays every year…'.

'Please,' replied Em, 'let's talk about something else shall we?' and then lightening her tone abruptly, 'Jodi's got a new job'.

Jodi Hayes, Em's old flatmate in Frithville Gardens had gone through RADA with her but for Jodi, the roles just did not materialise. She was attractive in a quirky sort of way with an engaging personality and a cheeky smile but for some reason, neither casting directors nor advertisers had taken to her. She got by temping and with the odd session behind a bar. Now it seemed things were looking up for her.

'So she's got a job as a junior presenter on local radio. It's a shame things didn't work out for her as an actor, but I think she'll be really good at this'. Indeed here, Em's prescience was spot on. Jodi quickly climbed the rungs of local radio, made the transition to terrestrial TV and now has her own show on Sky TV interviewing celebrities of all descriptions.

*

They returned from Malta to face a further three weeks of waiting before the series was to be aired. Three weeks filled with restlessness and anxiety, certainly on Em's part, and inevitably much of it rubbed off on Kay. She went back to working in the pub, never mentioning *The Broken Pane.* Inevitably, some of the customers knew, but whenever her acting career was mentioned, she or Kay, who frequently propped up the other side of the bar, would swiftly change the subject.

Finally, the big day arrived. Kay went to work as usual whilst Em stayed in bed. He had tried to talk to her but all he got were grunts and one-word answers.

It was common knowledge by now among Kay's colleagues that Em would be appearing on television that night. His closer friends understood the pressure that this had imposed upon them but for most, it was just a talking point and the opportunity to bathe in a little of her starlight, however faint.

Em refused point blank to watch episode one of the series and opted to take a shift in the pub which would have her working that evening. Kay however was determined to see the programme and settled down on the sofa at nine o'clock with a bottle of beer and a pizza.

Em did not appear until five minutes in but from then on he was transfixed. As in *The Doll's House*, he was not too interested in the plot, but concentrated purely on Em's performance.

Although they had lived together for some nine months, he found it easy to believe that she was not Em but Lucy Carter, a character who although born in London had moved with her family to the Devon/Dorset border country in her teens. However unqualified he was to judge, there was enough evidence here for him to believe that she had more than held her own. The other members of the cast passed him by as did the nuances of the plot but he was nonetheless disappointed when the first episode ended.

Immediately after the credits (which he noted had incorrectly spelled her surname with a 'y') he turned the television off and headed for The Princess Victoria. He entered the pub with a broad grin on his face. Em was standing behind the bar, dwarfed by the pub's high ceiling and met his glance with a worried, questioning expression. As soon as she had finished serving a customer he leaned across the bar and with genuine enthusiasm said quietly, 'Em, you were absolutely sensational!'

Somewhat surprisingly, her worried expression did not recede but instead, reaching between the beer pumps, took his hand and simply said, 'Thank you'. His support was a given but the real judgement on her performance would most likely come in the morning's newspapers.

They walked home in near silence and retired to bed with nothing more than a kiss. For much of the night, sleep eluded Kay, his thoughts constantly turning over what a series of negative reviews would mean to Em. He had experienced similar anxiety many years ago when waiting for his 'A' Level results. The tossing and turning to his right indicated that Em was going through a similar, although almost certainly more intense ordeal.

Chapter Sixteen

Tuesday 17th – Friday 20th May 2011

Kay got up early the next morning to buy every newspaper he could lay his hands on. He did not want Em to see any unfavourable reviews without his preparing her first. So, at six thirty he left the flat to walk the short distance to the newsagents near the station. The early rays of the sun were already promising a fine late Spring day. Despite the tender hour, the newsagent was awake enough to laugh at the number of papers Kay presented him with.

'Run out of toilet paper have you?' said the amiable Sikh behind the counter.

'Yes we're expecting an attack of dysentery,' replied Kay.

So, armed with nine papers with varying levels of intellectual content he returned to the flat and flicked through every paper in turn to see if there were any reviews of *The Broken Pane.* Indeed there were. The first he picked was *The Guardian* which had a couple of paragraphs. It was critical of the first episode in general, describing it as slow and a '*run of the mill production from the pen of Ian Hamilton*' but in a harbinger of things to come, it went on to say, '*…but Emma Silvester who plays Lucy Carter is a rare find. In an enchanting way she combines the* *poise of Helena Bonham-Carter with the working class sassiness of Sheridan Smith'.*

The Sun described her as '*stunning,*' the *Daily Mirror* as '*small but beautifully formed*'. The TV critic of the *Daily Telegraph* predicted a bright future for Em; '*The actress who portrays Lucy Carter (Emma Silvester) is clearly destined for much better things*'. The *Daily Mail* described her as, '*a tiny package bursting with talent*'. *The Times* broadly agreed with the *Telegraph*; '*Film Directors will be falling over each other to get her signature on their studios' contracts...*'.   There was however one tabloid that bucked the trend with, '*Emma Silvester is over-reaching herself as Lucy Carter*'. Kay could not understand how one paper could have such a different view from all the others and made a mental note to consign it to wrapping up potato peelings.

Just then his phone rang. It was his mother,

'Hi Kenny, saw Em on telly last night. Wasn't she *good.*'

'Yes,' replied Kay, 'but you try telling her that. She refused to watch it and is currently hiding under the bedclothes. I've been out to see if there were any reviews in the papers. There are, and with one exception they're all good'.

He quickly concluded the conversation with his mother and resolved to give Em the gist of the reviews.

'Come on starlet, wake up!' he shouted while shaking her vigorously by the shoulder, 'I've got some good news for you'.

Em opened her eyes. 'Go away. Leave me alone'.

'Like it or not, I'm going to read you some of the reviews. Now take your fingers out of your ears. One, *Emma Silvester... combines the poise of Helena Bonham-Carter with the working*

104

class sassiness of Sheridan Smith. Two*, Emma Silvester is destined for better things. Three…'* Kay gave her a precis of the reports from all the papers excluding of course, the errant tabloid that was even now in a pile of old papers earmarked for mundane domestic use.

'What?' said Em promptly changing her mood, 'let me see'.

Kay handed over the papers and so Em could read them for herself.

'Wow! I don't know what to say'.

'They love you. Next stop Hollywood…'.

Em got up as if in a trance, headed for the bathroom and when she emerged continued, 'I just can't believe they're saying those things about me'.

'Looks like you're going to be busy' said Kay glancing at her phone which was now sitting on the kitchen table. There were fourteen missed calls and thirty nine texts and it was still only eight fifteen.

*

Kay was late to work that morning but as soon as he arrived his colleagues all but formed a queue to tell him how they had seen Em in *The Broken Pane* last night and how good they thought she had been. Even sarcastic Nick was positive about her performance, 'Saw your bird on telly last night, thought she was pretty decent'. Mike on this occasion was restrained in his use of jargon and chipped in with, 'I have to say, she got all her ducks in a row with that performance'.

Although he was happy that Em's career was in the throes of taking a great leap forward, personally he felt something of a fraud, vicariously taking the praise from his colleagues resulting largely from the hard work and discipline of another human being. Kay knew that he had played his part, helping and encouraging her when things were at their bleakest but this was very small beer compared to the huge effort Em had put in herself.

At lunch, he tried his hardest to steer the conversation to anything but Em's performance in *The Broken Pane*. The football season was over now so that particular avenue was roadblocked and neither he nor any of his colleagues were hugely into cricket. In the end, he participated in a long discussion about Formula One Motor Racing, a sport in which he had even less interest than cricket but it did at least have the advantage of keeping the discussion on neutral ground.

All this may indicate that his mood was distinctly down but that was not so. Mentally, he was actually in a very good place and any drawbacks from Em's approaching celebrity status, if that is what it would be, could be parked for now. He was proud of her.

His journey home was almost entirely urban but for once he noticed that he was still in the midst of wildlife, not exactly nightingales in Berkeley Square but sparrows in Paddington and pigeons at Ladbroke Grove.

Not far from Shepherd's Bush, Em texted him to say that she was at her mother's house so as soon as he got home, he jumped into the Escort and drove to Mellitus Street. Although there was no chance of Ryan Browne being in the vicinity (he had been sentenced to nine months penal servitude and was in the early days of his sentence at The Mount), Kay was always wary getting out of his car on the Old Oak Estate. As soon as he entered the house, it was obvious that mother and daughter had been celebrating. There was an empty bottle of Prosecco lying on its side in the kitchen sink and they were well into a second by the evidence of the bottle on the living room table.

Kay felt as if he ought to join in but the presence of his car outside stayed his hand. He was unable to get much sense out of Em but it appeared that she had spent the day returning calls from friends and family, all of whom wished to congratulate her on her performance. It was mid-afternoon by the time she had completed this task and understandably she wanted to share her triumph with her mother. As the evening progressed, several neighbours dropped in followed by Jim on his return from work via the off-license and a regular party ensued.

The following day, Em awoke with what she described as the mother of all hangovers, so it was not until the evening that Kay managed to extract any sense out of her. It appeared that not only had she received any number of calls from those with whom she was acquainted on a social level but she had also received a call from Joanne. Joanne was Em's agent and although much of her call was congratulatory in tone, she also imparted the important information that she had received, quite separately, calls from two very influential people in the film world enquiring about Em's availability for the second half of the year. It was obvious that *The Broken Pane* had set a chain of events in motion, the outcome of which was not at that moment entirely clear but which had the potential to pluck Em from the relative obscurity of adverts and understudy roles and launch her on a trajectory which could place her in the front rank of actors of her generation.

*

Although it had been planned for some weeks, that Friday's meal with friends, Raj and Kate, Jayne and Dan and Jodi and her latest boyfriend, Lee, took on the semblance of a celebration. It was now impossible to steer the conversation away from Em and *The Broken Pane*. Kay looked around at the faces and was able to see the pleasure that mere mortals take in celebrity. It was new to him too but he had had months to get used to the possibility that Em would become little short of public property, a five foot nothing honeypot around which bees would from now on be constantly swarming.

On the next table, it seemed obvious that one, if not both of the elderly women seated there had seen *The Broken Pane*, recognised Em and were taking a keen interest in their conversation. Eventually, one of the women came over, 'Haven't I seen you on telly?' she asked, addressing Em.

'You may have done,' replied Em with a smile and perhaps the tiniest hint of conceit.

'Let me think, something to do with hairspray wasn't it? No shampoo! I thought you were very good'.

The whole table was laughing into their napkins as the woman slowly walked back to her table.

'To assume makes an ass out of u and me,' announced Kay quietly taking a quote straight out of Mike Hancock's phrase book.

Chapter Seventeen

For a little while, not much changed for Em and Kay. She continued to work shifts at The Princess Victoria, although her agent had advised her not to bother with any more auditions as there were plenty of enquiries coming in asking about her availability. She was now in the fortunate position of being able to choose her next step. Unfortunately for Kay however, it seemed that the sale of G & B had fallen through, or was at least taking longer than had been expected, so he still put in daily appearances at the office near Moorgate. His job also included frequent trips to see clients at various locations throughout southern England and these outings varied from high level interrogations to glorified piss-ups. It was during one of the latter that Kay received a message from Em; _'Been offered another job. Looks good. Talk to you later. Xxxxx'_.

The role Em had been offered involved playing the joint lead in a sitcom for the BBC. There were to be six episodes, all being filmed between August and November with screening scheduled for early in the new year. _Herbert Square_ had been described to Em as 'Eastenders with laughs'.

In truth, accepting the offer took little thought especially as the payment she would receive was a large multiple of that she received for *The Broken Pane*. Again, Em's life would revolve around the reading of scripts and from 8th August, early starts and late finishes. One issue that Em had to face up to was that filming was to be in Borehamwood and as yet, she had no driving license. She had already taken her test once, resulting in a narrow failure and had another booked for June 16th. It was not impossible to get to the studios by train but it would make it so much easier if she could drive. In addition to formal lessons, Kay regularly took her out for driving practice even though the high levels of traffic in West London could definitely be unnerving for a novice driver. Jim also volunteered to help but given that this would involve a 3-litre Capri of considerable vintage, the offer was politely declined.

Fortunately, Em managed to pass her driving test on the second attempt. One week's pay from *Herbert Square* would have paid for a pretty decent vehicle but the parking situation in Coverdale Road was such that a car each was simply unconscionable. So, the poor old Escort with 96,000 miles on the clock would once again be pressed into service.

The fact that the first month's filming was taking place during school holidays made the journey to Borehamwood, almost exactly due north, a lot easier for Em than would normally have been the case. But once the schools were back and the roads once again gridlocked, her inexperience meant that there was a high chance that at some stage she would have the odd scrape.

As it happened, the incident near Gipsy Corner on the early evening of Friday October 21st was a little more than that. Kay was already home watching television with the dinner quietly simmering in the kitchen when Em shamefacedly entered the flat. He had only to take one look at her to realise something was wrong.

'…had a bit of an accident,' she said, staring at the floor.

'Why, what's happened? Are you okay?'

'Yes but the car's not,'

Kay looked at her, rolled his eyes, opened the door into the corridor and in a deliberately measured fashion, descended the stairs. There on the side of the street was the Escort looking very much the worse for wear. The bonnet was bent, the number plate hanging by one screw and the off-side headlight was smashed. In fact the whole of the front showed considerable damage, which Kay quickly realised was likely to cost more to repair than the car was worth.

Em was clearly shaken so, biting his tongue a little, he just said, 'So long as you're all right, that's all that matters'.

'How can you be so calm,' Em replied, 'I've just wrecked your car!'

'I know, but it's only a car' was Kay's response.

Underneath, Kay was a lot more upset than he was letting on. All right, cars were not one of his great passions but he had had this one for nearly ten years and there was something about owning a car that nobody could possibly lust after that summed up his attitude to material possessions in general. It was all very well for Tony to own a Maserati and a Range Rover, as well as an E-type Jag for summer Sundays but Kay did not envy Tony one iota. Their outlooks on life were polar opposites. He could afford Tony some respect for his efforts in building up G & B into one of the country's largest independent insurance brokers but there was precious little about his lifestyle that Kay would want to emulate. Right there and then, he resolved that whatever the cost, the car *was* going to be repaired. Notwithstanding his attitude to possessions, he could see that this course of action would also help to rebuild Em's probably shattered confidence in showing her that despite the damage, ultimately the thing was repairable.

Without letting on to Em, he phoned Jim and got the name of a bodywork specialist just off Acton Vale.

*

Eddie Marsh was one of those down to earth, permanently dirty, chain-smoking individuals in which the motor trade abounds.

'What do you want me to do with this then?' asked Eddie followed by a lung-busting cough.

'Could you fix it for me. Please,' replied Kay putting the stress on the 'please'.

'Fucking thing's not worth it. Just take the insurance money and get a new one'.

'Jim Lascelles said you'd help me out. I know it's really not worth doing but I have my reasons'.

Eddie gave Kay a sideways glance, shook his head and tutted. 'It'll need a new bumper, new grille, headlamp's fucked. Might be able to knock the dent out of that wing, not sure about the bonnet but it's going to cost you a shedload of money and it'll take time. I wouldn't do it, but Jim's a good lad and I owe him a favour or two'.

'I'd be really grateful if you could.'

Eddie thought for a minute, coughed again, blew his nose on a filthy rag and then said, 'All right. Bring it in, not next week but the one after and I'll see what I can do'.

'Thanks,' said Kay with a sigh, 'Would Wednesday do?'

'Yeah.'

As Kay was leaving he could hear Eddie say under his breath, 'One born every fucking minute'.

Kay didn't care. This was far more than simply an old jalopy.

For a few days, Em had to take the train until one of the studio technicians who lived in Hammersmith offered to give her a lift. Filming was long over by the time the Escort was finally repaired which was something of a nuisance to Kay. Since early that Spring, he had encouraged Em to accompany him to the countryside whenever they could find time. He was not a townie, he told himself and needed regular access to open fields and woodland to keep on the level. It was not worth hiring a car simply for these jaunts so during the late Autumn, he simply had to go without.

Chapter Eighteen

Wednesday November 4th 2011

Kay had never really been the sort to maintain regular contact with old school friends. In fact he could only think of two whose whereabouts were known to him – Rick Weldon who was now a chartered accountant in Oxford and Craig Jones, who after flirting with the world of advertising had ultimately become a history teacher in Witney. His best friend from this time however was Paul Maisey. After taking his 'A' Levels, Paul had dived straight into the world of work whilst most of his contemporaries had opted for university, thus putting off the evil day for another three years. Kay and Paul had remained in contact for a while but over time their correspondence had petered out and it was a good twelve years since Kay had heard from Paul.

It was thus totally unexpected when, walking down Regent Street after a client visit in the West End, Kay spotted a once familiar face in the crowd near Oxford Circus Station. Paul saw Kay at virtually the same time and smiled.

'Hey Paul, how you doing old friend, haven't seen you for years!' said Kay.

'Kay old son, it must be ten, twelve years. How you going?'

To avoid the crush they pulled over to stand by a shop window. The two men shook hands and looked each other up and down. From Paul's manner of dress, it was obvious that he was a fish out of water in this present location. He was clothed entirely in a drab green, his sweater a little paler than either trousers or jacket while his footwear was designed for coping with mud rather than the pavements of Central London.

'Let's have a beer,' said Kay, 'have you got time?'

'I'm free all afternoon,' replied Paul.

Kay, being far more on home turf than Paul, took the lead and headed northward along Upper Regent Street, then took a right along Margaret Street. Arriving at The Cock Tavern, Kay pushed the door open and entered the crowded, mahogany clad bar room. Every seat in the place was taken and so after getting served they stood clutching pint glasses mid-way between the bar and the row of occupied tables ranged against the wall. Paul was first to start a conversation, 'So what you been up to these last twelve years?'.

Kay gave Paul a potted history of his life since leaving school. His old friend was particularly impressed that Kay's partner was an actress some ten years his junior; 'Sounds like you've landed on your feet there old pal. Jeez old Kay Nettleton shacked up with an actress!' he said shaking his head.

At length, Kay drew to a close and said, 'Well, that's my life in a nutshell, how about you? I guess from this getup that the West End is not your normal stamping ground'.

'Well observed,' I'm only here for an interview at the BBC,'. He laughed as it became clear that Kay's mind had immediately jumped to the occasion some six years before when one Guy

Goma had arrived for a job interview and due to a mix-up of thermonuclear proportions had been thrust in front of the cameras on live TV, mistaken for an expert on technical litigation in the music industry.

'Actually I was here to record an interview on the possibility of re-introducing the white stork to the UK'.

Kay's ears pricked up. It was obvious that Paul spoke his language.

'After I left school, I drifted from job to job, the usual sort of stuff; bar work, labourer on a building site, that sort of thing. Then I met this girl, Pia was her name, she was a ranger for the National Trust in Sussex. She told me about her life dealing with nature in the raw, so to speak. We immediately clicked and it was as if a fog had been lifted. I knew what I wanted to do'.

They sat down as the lunchtime rush subsided and a table became free.

'I applied for one job after another and finally landed one on a large nature reserve in North Wales. It was simply a 'gopher' job; go for this, go for that, and the money was a pittance but I had my foot in the door. Not long after joining I started a degree course in Conservation and Environmental Management, passed that and then spent two years on a project in British Columbia.

I came back to this country in 2005, worked my bollocks off and now you see me as the newly appointed director of a wildlife trust in the West Country'.

Kay was enthralled but couldn't help picking up on one point that had been left hanging.

'And what happened to Pia?'

'Buggered if I know. We went out for a while, had a bit, actually quite a lot of how's your father, as you do, and then somehow lost contact when she took up a post in the Hebrides. Christ, was she hot between the sheets... But that's all in the past. I got married to Anna three years ago and we've now got an eighteen-month old boy, imaginatively called Paul'.

Kay listened politely to Paul's descriptions of his home life with Anna, made the right noises in the right places but his mind was already elsewhere, out in the fields and the forests with the deer and the ravens.

One pint turned into two, then three, then to even it up, four... After a while Kay thought it politic to go outside and phone the office saying he had a stomach upset and was going home. He had no meetings that afternoon so little damage was done. Despite his increasingly fuzzy head it became clear to him that Paul was somebody with whom he really needed to keep in contact. They swapped numbers and rather unsteadily went their separate ways. As luck would have it, the route for both of them went via Paddington Station where they parted with a man-hug and a mutual 'Stay in touch'.

His arrival in Coverdale Road was not actually any later than usual so he thought he would sit down and watch television for a minute... Suddenly he realised that Em was standing over him with a face like thunder. Bewildered, he fielded questions like 'Where's the dinner?' and 'Have you been drinking?' followed by blunt statements such as 'You're too pissed, I'll get it myself'. Eventually it dawned on him that Em was not best pleased with his behaviour.

Kay tried to explain whom he had met and why it was important but either Em was not in listening mode or his words were too slurred to make much sense. By the end of the evening however, she had calmed down enough to make civil conversation and he had sobered up sufficiently to give her a resumé of his day.

Thoroughly sober by the time he went to bed, he lay awake going over and over his meeting with Paul and what it might mean for his future.

Chapter Nineteen

November 2011

Filming had finished in the second week of November and although it was far from holiday season, Kay proposed that they take a short holiday in East Devon. This was very much because he fancied the idea of bird watching on the river estuaries between Lyme Regis and Torquay. In any event, Em did not seem to mind and was even beginning to show some small degree of enthusiasm for the nature trips that Kay insisted on taking when he could find the time.

They stayed in a pub in Topsham, on the Exe estuary and a noted spot for bird watching. Whilst Em had begun to get some idea of the birds she was likely to encounter in jaunts to the Chilterns or the North Downs, even recognising some of their calls, here it was obvious that she found herself all at sea. It was one thing to tell the difference between say, a blue tit and a great tit but a bar tailed godwit and a black tailed godwit? Even Kay struggled with that one. Nonetheless, the teal and the oyster catcher were both enchanting and quite distinctive. And the plaintive call of the curlew had clearly captivated her.

But the highlight of their trip was the sight of an adult dog otter bounding along carrying a fish on the mudflats almost under their noses.

'You know Kay, you're not like anybody I've ever known,' said Em in the bar that evening.

'How do you mean?' he replied.

'You think about things. You care. And you do things which defy logic.'

'I'm not sure I buy that one. Explain?'

'So we both know that you could afford a much better car, maybe not a Ferrari but say, a decent BMW but you insist on pouring money into an old banger. Most people I know would move heaven and Earth to get their hands on a decent car'.

'Jim has old cars.'

'That's completely different. He buys them cheap, does them up a bit and sells them at a profit. It's part of his lifestyle. And it's not only cars, it's what you wear too. You buy cheap clothes from chains and turn your nose up at designer labels.'

'That's because they're a complete waste of money, you're just buying the name. But why are you complaining about me? Why now?'

'It's not a complaint. It really isn't. It's part of the Kay that I love. It would be different if you were mean, but you're not. You're actually very generous. You're just... different'.

'And is that bad?'

'No, of course not, silly. I was just pointing out that if it were me, I'd have a BMW Z4, Gucci shoes, Versace knickers...'.

'I don't care what knickers you wear, it's what's underneath that counts'.

She gave him a mock reproachful look, 'Shall we go upstairs?'.

'I think we should'.

*

Kay had never been particularly fond of beach holidays but in his teenage years, there were many advantages to following the trend, not least for the girls you could meet. But now in his thirties he was less keen. Summer holidays he felt, could be just too crowded. A vacation in November or the three months following Christmas gave you more peace and the opportunity to really get to know someone, or if you knew them, then to get to know them *better*.

It disappointed him that Em seemed to hanker after the geegaws of wealth. He would be happy enough if she wanted a nice house, well-made furniture and art to hang on the walls but the things she professed to want were in footballers' wives territory. The irony that he had nearly been a professional footballer was not lost on Kay. Perhaps it was a reaction to her tough upbringing and not having much that she could call her own as a child. Was he being a snob? Probably, but he reflected that neither of his parents came from a privileged background. Nonetheless, he felt a little uneasy with himself for thinking that way. With the income that she would receive from *Herbert Square* however, she would soon be able to buy, within reason, pretty much anything she wanted. Was it any of his business to try and influence how she spent her money?

One thing they had already decided on, and Kay was very much in favour of, was a move to a more desirable location. The best flats got snapped up almost in the blinking of an eye and so they agreed that when they got back they would take a few days out to look in the more up-market parts of West London, finally settling on a first floor flat in Thornton Avenue, just round the corner from Turnham Green Station.

Chapter Twenty

February – March 2012

The first episode of *Herbert Square* was screened on Tuesday February 7th and the series would continue until March 13th. The reviews were generally favourable and once again the critics were kind to Em. In a *volte face* of epic proportions, the very same tabloid that had described Em as over-reaching herself reported, '*After her triumph in The Broken Pane, Emma Silvester has proved that she is every bit as effective in comedy as she is in straight drama*'.

Joanne was again kept busy fielding enquiries as to Em's availability but her advice this time was to sit tight and be choosy.

The first thing Em did choose to do was a commercial for a major clothing retailer. This wasn't just being a pretty face in the background but a full speaking part in which her personality was central to the whole advert. From her point of view this commercial had two major factors in its favour. Firstly, it didn't take very long to do and secondly it paid her money, shedloads of it.

Despite his misgivings, Kay congratulated her on her good taste when a larger proportion of this money than one might expect found its way into her wardrobe. He reasoned that she was young and the phase may pass, but then again it may not…

A perhaps more understandable manifestation of Em's new found affluence came later that month when they were sitting at the table eating dinner.

'Kay…' Em said in a tone that started his alarm bells ringing, '… I know you've had your car for ten or however many years it may be and you're very fond of it, but don't you think it's about time we bought a new one?' Kay had been expecting this and, to tell the truth, he knew that in the end he would have to accede but he thought he would string her along for a bit.

'Yes, I think you're right. There's a guy at work who's got a five year old Skoda for sale. It's only done twenty five thou…

'Kay, are you pissing me about. I don't want a five year old Skoda'.

'Oh, okay… I did see a nice Fiesta in a second hand car lot in Brentford the other day'.

'Kay!! I don't want a fucking second hand Fiesta.' She paused, 'You are, you're taking the piss out of me!'.

'Me? Would I do that?'

She reached onto the sofa for a cushion and hit Kay over the head with it.

'You're supposed to be the actor, couldn't you see I was winding you up?' he laughed as another blow from the cushion landed on his shoulder.

'You're taking the piss out of me, you evil man!' repeated Em as she continued to swipe at him with the cushion, while Kay shook with laughter.

Despite the knockabout nature of this discussion, Kay really did have severe misgivings about a novice driver taking to the road with machinery that in all probability was way beyond their ability to control. Although she had a Porsche or perhaps an Audi TT in mind, he knew Em well enough to believe that she would eventually see sense and opt for something more suited to her inexperience. In the end, the compromise came in the form of an eighteen month old Alfa Romeo, the least powerful in the range but with sufficient cachet to satisfy Em. Much to Kay's regret, the Balham based car dealer who sold it to them took the Escort in part-exchange. Kay had owned this car through the good times and the bad and he almost felt as if some part of him had died when he left it in the uncaring hands of the dealer.

*

Offers of work were now coming in thick and fast for Em. She opted to do another advert, this time for a Japanese motor manufacturer. Again, her bank balance swelled in response. This was followed by a voice-over for coffee - a couple of days work and another boost to her deposit account.

Then on March 7th, Joanne phoned her to say that she thought there was something really special in the offing. Apparently, she had been phoned the previous day by a woman working in conjunction with Monty McLay, the well-known film director whose CV included *The Three Titans, North of Eden* and a dramatization of the Dickens classic, *Hard Times*. The main thrust of the call was to check on what sort of fee Em would expect for a major supporting role in his next film to be shot in the Caribbean over the summer.

'She told her £200,000 should just about cover it,' Em told Kay over dinner.

Kay nearly choked on his lasagne and sat there open-mouthed for a full twenty seconds.

'Wow, just wow,' managed Kay once he had recovered his composure. 'I told you you'd be a big star'.

'Hang on, I haven't got it yet,' replied Em, 'and it's not really a starring role. Joanne might have asked for too much but she did say that the woman wasn't fazed by the figure'.

'Did she say anything about the film?' said Kay eager to find out more.

'Yeah, a bit. It's called *The Plantation* and is a historical drama set in Barbados in the early nineteenth century and I guess the background theme will be slavery. Monty McLay is a Scottish director who mostly does historical dramas. He hasn't been around for that long but is really making a name for himself. I guess he's probably not much older than you. Do you remember *The Three Titans*?'

'Yes, I think so. Set in Ancient Greece or somewhere wasn't it?'

'Rome' replied Em displaying her historical knowledge. 'It was a kind of *Cleopatra* with a grain of truth and the right coloured people. I can even tell you the names of the three titans.'

'Go on then smart arse.'

'They were were Octavian, Pompey and Mark Anthony.'

'I'm impressed,' said Kay.

'I liked history at school and it might have helped that I was an extra on the film during my time at RADA.'

The last few months had brought Em unbridled success so she took the wait in her stride. Yes, the money was great but if it didn't come off, there appeared to be plenty of other opportunities for her, since her name was now obviously known in all the right places. In the event, Joanne confirmed that a formal offer was going to be made with no significant reduction in the payment she had suggested.

Of the two however, it was Kay who was more on edge about it, not so much whether Em landed the role or not but more about the three months she would have to spend in the Caribbean. Although he never mentioned this to Em, he would have been happier if she had continued to be cast in roles filmed in this country. There was, of course, no way he would or should interfere. He took the view, as he had all along, that Em's career was completely outside his control and what would be would be.

In addition to offers of work, Em was also beginning to get requests from various media organisations for her to give interviews. She resisted all of these for as long as she could but in the end gave first refusal to Jodi who jumped at the chance to interview somebody who was already on the foothills of becoming a household name.

As one would expect, the interview was largely conducted in a friendly and light-hearted manner, ranging over her childhood, her time at RADA and her breakthrough in the business. Em even found time to thank Kay for his patience and support over the last two years. The only part of the interview that found Em on the back foot concerned her late father. It would have been obvious to the listener that Jodi, despite being Em's friend, had touched a raw nerve.

After listening to the interview on the radio, Kay mentioned that she had sounded uncomfortable when the subject was raised.

'I know,' she replied, 'but it's something I'll have to come to terms with. It wasn't Jodi's fault, she's a journalist now and has to get under the skin of her interviewees or else her career will go tits up. I just wish my family background was as uncomplicated as yours Kay that's all'.

Chapter Twenty One

April 2012

At the beginning of April, Kay came in one morning to the news that Jayne had handed in her notice. To most of her colleagues this was no great surprise but it did seem rather sudden, especially as there was still the likelihood that G & B would be sold with the possibility of a substantial pay off. She had as yet not revealed the details of the rumours she had heard but the inference was, of course, that Tony was implicated in something unspeakable. It was clear to all around her that whenever he emerged from his office, Jayne made sure that she was nowhere to be seen.

The news seemed to put Tony into a state of high agitation. He mislaid more files than normal, shouted at his junior staff more frequently and drank more whisky in the seclusion of his office than ever before.

Jayne had sent her resignation to Mike by email which started the rumour mill working at a furious pace. No more would she be seen at the offices of Gresham & Bailey. Kay sent her a text to try and establish what was going on and got the following reply;

'It's a rather sordid story. If we can meet up sometime I'll tell you the gory details, perhaps Raj would like to come too. Not sure I'd want Nick and his lot to know though. Jayne x'.

They met a couple of days later in the Olde Cheshire Cheese in Fleet Street which had plenty of tables in the cellar where they could sit and talk with some degree of privacy.

'So, it was like this,' said Jayne, 'I was working overtime on the Hinckley Electronics deal and I'd just gone to the kitchen to make a cup of coffee. It was late and I was tired so I didn't hear him come in. Anyway, I heard a sound and looked round but there was nobody there, so I carried on making my coffee. A couple of seconds later he – Tony - grabbed me from behind and squeezed my breasts to the point where it actually hurt. I was absolutely petrified. I screamed but there was nobody there to hear. And all the time he was telling me I was beautiful and how he had admired me ever since I joined the company and if I consented to sex with him how much good it would do my career, or words to that effect'.

'What an absolute cunt,' said Raj.

'But it didn't end there,' Jayne continued. 'I recovered my composure, jabbed my elbow backwards right into his midriff, he grunted and let go. I turned round, his flies were open and he was well… exposed'.

'So what did you do then?' asked Kay aghast.

'I picked up the first thing I could lay my hands on, which happened to be the washing up brush and hit it as hard as I could. He screamed and I just fled from the building.

When I got back home and told Dan, he was all for hunting him down and all but murdering the bastard but I told him that all that would do was put him in jail'.

The group went silent for a few seconds and then then Jayne continued,

'The following day, the day I handed in my notice, I went to see a solicitor, there didn't seem much point in involving the police at that stage. She advised me that it would be impossible to prove anyway as there were no witnesses but she did say that I should try to find out if anybody else in the company had had a similar experience.

I've been talking to Gill who's been there pretty much since G & B was founded. She told me that there'd been a woman working there seven or eight years ago called Samantha Mepham who left suddenly, accusing Tony of assault, but again there was no evidence and it never got to court. Gill's still in touch with her and suggested that we meet up. She was apparently really keen to meet me and I'm seeing her next week. I'm really determined to give Tony what's coming to him however long it takes. Anyway, revenge is a dish best served cold'. She paused for a second, 'Look, I'm telling you all this in confidence. I really don't want it to go any further, the last thing I want is for it to get back to him'.

'What will you do now?' said Raj.

'I've not been happy at work for a long time, I don't think I can stick insurance any longer. By and large the people are great but the work is mind-numbing. I've been considering moving into the law and seeing how far that takes me. Perhaps this will give me the impetus I need'.

Jayne looked at her watch, 'Anyway, I must be going now, I've got to meet Dan. Thanks for listening.'

With that, she kissed each of them in turn and disappeared up the stairs. Kay looked at Raj, 'Phew that was heavy. I never liked Tony much, nobody does, but I never thought he was capable of that.'

Raj shook his head, 'if it wasn't somebody I knew, I would take it with a pinch of salt but it's Jayne and I believe her one hundred percent'.

After another pint they walked out of the pub into the little court, turned left and then left again into Fleet Street.

'You know, there's one more thing that worries me,' said Raj, 'the following day. We must have washed our cups up with that brush!'

Chapter Twenty Two

May – August 2012

The days counting down to Em's departure for Barbados passed remarkably quickly. She was no longer working in the pub and so tended to lunch with friends as often as possible. Learning the script accounted for a good part of her time whilst much of the remainder was spent at a gym which she religiously attended out of fear that she might put on weight before filming began.

Kay had bought Em many presents before, but this one, which had not cost much was simply intended to make her laugh. You can find almost anything on the internet if you try and, after much searching, he found the very thing. The day it arrived, he carefully wrapped it as if it were a game of pass the parcel and gave it to her over dinner. Em eagerly opened the package, strewing wrapping paper left, right and centre. Eventually she had torn off sufficient paper to reveal a small box. The box contained a pair of earrings each one bearing the enamel image of a small bird.

'Go on, now tell me what they are,' he said playfully.

'Well, they're earrings,' she replied somewhat mystified.

'No you numpty, what species!'

'Blue tits? No, great tits. So…'

There was a pause until, suddenly, she twigged.

'They're not that big,' she laughed looking down at her breasts.

Kay raised an eyebrow. 'Take it how you like, but 'great' can also mean very good, excellent as in Alexander the Great. Qualitative not quantitative.'

'You clown! But I'll treasure them wherever I go'. She put them on then turned and kissed him, 'fortunately none of my friends are bird watchers, otherwise I'd have some explaining to do'.

*

Meanwhile, Kay's work at Gresham & Bailey continued as depressingly as before, until abruptly on 14 May all the staff were called into Meeting Room 1, the largest room in the office. Despite the room's size, Kay found that he, together with at least half the employees had to string themselves out around the edge. Tony was sitting at the front along with a sharp-suited man that Kay didn't recognise. After a lot of coughing and whispered conversation amongst the gathered throng, Tony opened the meeting by introducing the man as Roger Luffman, Chief Executive of Levison Drake plc.

Kay's opinion of his boss had never been high but ever since Jayne's revelations, he found it difficult to approach anything he did in a positive light. After a minor glitch with the PowerPoint presentation, Tony continued with the words, 'Some of you may be aware that talks have been going on…', followed by a lot of waffle that Kay instantly forgot. Getting more into his stride,

Tony put great emphasis on the phrase 'significant opportunity' followed, a little while later by 'greater market penetration of the merged company' and more importantly to Kay's ears, 'economies of scale'.

The thrust of Tony's speech was that, as predicted, G & B was to be sold. The unspoken subtext was that Tony was going to benefit hugely from the deal and he really didn't care much what anybody else thought.

After a quarter of an hour or so, Tony blathered to a halt with the words, 'I would now like to hand you over to Mr. Roger Luffman to flesh out some of the finer points of the merger. Roger…'.

The CEO of Levison Drake turned out to be almost as oily as Tony. There were great opportunities (he said) for those who wanted to stay with the company but there was some duplication of roles and, under pressure he admitted that there would be a number of redundancies. Kay kept his own counsel, just hoping that his role would be one of those that Luffman wished to dispense with. 'Of course, we will take people's preferences into account' said Luffman. 'Yeah, if it suits you,' thought Kay.

After the meeting, Raj sought Kay out and quietly said, 'You won't catch me working for that slimeball. What a creep. Makes Tony look like Nelson Mandela'. Although the overstatement was obvious, it was clear that Raj and Kay were of one mind with regard to the merits of Levison Drake's CEO.

On the Wednesday of that week, Kay had a meeting with Mike Hancock.

'So going forward, what did you take away from the meeting on Monday, Kay?' Mike opened.

'Well, going forward, a pencil and an A4 pad, I believe Mike. I didn't think you'd noticed'.

Mike gave him a long if hardly piercing stare. That was a level of piss-taking too unsubtle for even Mike not to twig. After a pause he continued,

'There has been a paradigm shift in the business. Call Monday ground zero. Where do you see your career progression from that point in time'.

'Oh God…' thought Kay and countered, 'Well frankly Mike, I would like to bite the bullet. Can you run it up the flagpole with your new masters and give me the lowdown?'

'Of course,' said Mike, apparently impressed with Kay's mastery of gobbledygook, 'but I'm not sure you're in one of the categories we wish to put out to grass'.

*

The following week, Mike called Kay into one of the meeting rooms and handed him a piece of paper with a figure on it. It said £19,267.14. This was roughly in line with what Kay had expected but unusually they wanted him to work his notice. This meant another three months doing a job that he had grown to despise. He figured however that they could hardly expect him to work flat out during that period and the technique would be to stay just the right side of the mark. By and large he had toed the line during his employment with G & B, not taken overly long lunchbreaks, excessive days off sick or put soap in Tony's coffee (he had put it in Nick's instead) and so his brownie points total should be fairly heavily in credit. He would, it seemed, have to do something pretty heinous for the offer of cash to be withdrawn.

It has to be said though that after he had formally accepted the offer, his lunchbreaks got markedly longer and he did take a couple of days off with sticky mattress syndrome.

*

Finally, the day came for Em to depart for Bridgetown. Kay took her and a case, which completely dwarfed her, to Heathrow Airport for the 11.54 flight. It was raining and the traffic on the M25 was particularly bad that morning. Fortunately, Kay had some experience of getting to Heathrow in the early morning and had left plenty of time for a cup of coffee once Em had checked in. Looking him in the eyes, she promised to write to him at least every day and their goodbye kiss lasted a full five minutes. Just as she was about to go through the departure gate, she reached into her hand luggage and pulled out a cardboard tube which she gave to him. 'Don't open it until you get home,' she said with a twinkle in her eye.

A soon as he got back to the flat he took a rolled up piece of paper out of the tube and laid it out on the table. Kay smiled, it was an extremely well-drawn nude executed rather in the style of Édouard Manet's *Olympia*. The features however were obviously Em's. With it was a large yellow Post-it Note on which she had written in very small handwriting, *'This was drawn a couple of years ago by a student at The Slade. It's very lifelike don't you think? I want you to have it to remind you of*

me while I'm away. All my love darling. Em'. This simple
message was then followed by no less than fourteen x's.

*

Em's first text message was sent very shortly after her plane
touched down at Grantley Adams International Airport;

*Arrived safely. Film company sent a posh car to pick me up.
Staying in a really nice hotel overlooking the beach. Bit tired.
All my love darling xxxxx.*

The Olympics were due to start in six weeks' time and the
whole of London was abuzz with expectation. If nothing else, it
was something to distract him from the crossroads that, now in
his mid-thirties, his life had reached. There were any number of
leaving drinks to attend as various employees of what was now
officially called Levison Drake (G & B Division) Ltd. took the
money and ran. Raj had also taken redundancy and celebrated by
announcing that in the new year, he would marry his long-term
partner Kate which of course, was the excuse for another drink.

As soon as the takeover had been announced, Raj had started
hunting for another job and within two weeks had been offered,
and accepted, a fairly senior middle-management position with a
large insurance company based in Manchester. It would mean
moving but housing in the north was not as expensive as in the
London suburbs and Raj anticipated being able to buy a far
better house than would have been possible had he stayed in the
south.

Kay had decided to use the summer for rest and relaxation before making any final decisions about his future. For a start, Em was away in the Caribbean and he knew he had to involve her in the decision-making process but making far-reaching decisions by phone and email was really not satisfactory. Besides, he had worked solidly since leaving university fourteen years ago and he thought he owed it to himself to have a little break from the grindstone of work.

Em's texts continued to come in at the rate of two and sometimes three a day. According to her the leading man, a prominent American actor was a bit of a perfectionist with a very short fuse and hence was a real nightmare to work with. Monty however, was a real sweetie who ensured that the cast's every whim was catered for. She was getting sufficient time off to just chill out on the beach in the company of the other actors and crew members. Kay was envious, but only up to a point. Barbados sounded great but the temperatures and the strength of sun likely to be experienced in a West Indian summer were way beyond the levels he would find comfortable, even if the outside possibility of a hurricane might tickle his sense of adventure.

*

Fortunately for Kay, his redundancy money came through a day before the three months were up and as he was no longer beholden to G & B, he resolved to play a little trick on his boss. Part of the takeover agreement was that Tony would stay on for a period of twelve months as a consultant, although in actual practice he would only come in once or twice a week.

Nonetheless, this meant that his office remained unchanged. On Kay's official last day, he came in with a roll of Gaffer tape and a kipper that he had bought from a Tesco Express en route. There was nobody around at lunchtime, or at least nobody who would split on him. Making sure the coast was clear, he sneaked into Tony's office, slid under his smart mahogany desk and with the Gaffer tape, attached the kipper to the underside of the leather coated desktop. Given Jayne's revelations, Kay felt that he deserved infinitely worse than this. It was a shame that he wasn't going to be around to witness the results but it still made him feel that he had taken a small step on the way to paying Tony back for the indignities he had inflicted on his staff over the last few years.

Chapter Twenty Three

Thursday 23rd – Friday 24th August 2012

Kay was worried. He hadn't heard from Em for more than a day.
This was unusual and when the message did finally come
through thirty six hours later, all it said was;

*Sorry haven't written. Been very busy. Things going well. Hope
all ok with you. Xxx*

Perhaps he was reading too much into things. Not having her
there upset the rhythm of his life; perhaps she *was* very busy and
the filming was making her tired but previous texts had stressed
how much fun she was having. It seemed, well, *odd*.

On his first day of liberty, he decided he would drive out to
Amersham to see his parents. His father would be at work but as
it was during school holidays, both his mother and Jack would
be there and doubtless his father would appear later. The weather
was pleasant, if not blazing hot; certainly nothing like as hot as it
would have been for Em in the Caribbean.

There was a family issue to discuss and his mother had been
asking him to call in for a week or two. His grandfather, old
Manny Weissman, was becoming increasingly vague and had
had a series of falls in his Ealing home, a late nineteenth century
building of much charm but very little practicality for someone

well into their ninth decade. Kay's grandmother, Edna had died while he was at university and since that time Manny had lived alone with his memories, good and bad, and the odd visit from neighbours and family. Now it looked as if the time had come for him to move into accommodation more appropriate to his age.

Ruth did not particularly want Kay to get involved in the nitty-gritty of choosing a retirement home for the old man, she simply wanted a sounding board, somebody to okay the decisions she and her surviving sister had, as near as dammit, already made. As such his opinion was actually irrelevant but he knew that it would make his mother feel better to have his support so he carefully looked through the brochures he was handed and agreed, as he knew he would, that his mother had made a wise choice.

'How's Em getting on?' enquired Ruth when they had finished discussing retirement homes.

'Okay,' Kay replied, but there was something in his tone that alerted her to the fact that he was concerned. She knew, and that indefinable link between mother and son also meant that he knew she knew.

'I'm sure she's very busy,' said Ruth, and now it was his turn to pick up on the concern in her voice that she had attempted to hide.

Jack had cycled to the park to play football with friends and was not expected back until five o'clock or later, his timekeeping frequently causing friction with his mother. Despite having signed a schoolboy contract with Reading Football Club, Jack still spent much of his spare time kicking a football around any available patch of grass. His parents were secretly pleased however that he didn't spend all his spare time cloistered in his bedroom playing computer games like so many of his contemporaries.

He sloped in just before six o'clock, receiving a 'What time do you call this?' look from Ruth.

'I guess you don't want a game of football now?' laughed Kay.

'I will after dinner.' Jack's voice had begun to break and he was now every bit a teenager with the beginnings of acne and attitude.

Richard returned from London at six forty five and slumped into a chair. He was at that stage in his career when he so wanted to retire but couldn't quite afford to do so if he wished to maintain his lifestyle. Every day at work was therefore purgatory for him. They had two grandchildren but given their location on the other side of the world, he and Ruth rarely saw them. They weren't due to fly out until the following year and so had to make do with regular telephone calls, but it just wasn't the same.

'Glass of beer!' said Richard suddenly. He jumped up, headed for a cupboard in the utility room and pulled out a bottle of Timothy Taylor's Landlord. 'Want one Kay?'

'Go on then.' Richard reached in for another bottle.

The beer was a little too warm but that was rather better than having it frozen to death in the refrigerator.

'What are you going to do now you're a man of leisure?' Richard ventured.

'I don't know yet. Anything but insurance broking,' replied Kay defensively.

'Well don't leave it too long, you'll get rusty.'

After dinner, Kay had a brief kick about with Jack but as the late summer light was beginning to fade, the game had to be curtailed after half an hour or so.

Just after he had returned to Turnham Green, Kay received another text from Em; *Things going well here. Hope all okay with you. Can we talk? xxx*

This looked ominous. No 'missing you', no expressions of love. The first two brief sentences were the sort of bland statements you would add to a post card reluctantly written to your great aunt, not a lover of more than two years standing.

Kay attempted to call Em but was not able to get through. It was gone twelve now and despite his highly agitated condition, he decided to retire to bed. This proved to be a bad idea. An hour passed without the least hint of his falling asleep. It would still be only eight thirty in Barbados he told himself, so he decided to try again. Still no connection. Half an hour later he attempted to call for a third time. Same result.

He turned on the television halfway through some awful low budget movie and watched the film sporadically without grasping the slightest hint of the plot. Every half hour he would attempt to phone Em. At four o'clock he gave up, turned the television off and went back to bed.

This time, he did sleep intermittently but his rest was interrupted by a dream in which he was constantly searching for Em but without success. At last, he saw her in the distance but she drifted out of sight when he approached, not to be seen again before he awoke.

He managed to sleep until eight and then, as no further sleep seemed likely, headed to the bathroom for a shower. There would be no point in trying to phone Em until at least mid-day and even then given the filming schedule, she might be unable to take the call.

As it happened, he didn't need to call her because at just gone twelve thirty his phone rang. It was Em.

'Hi Sweetheart,' said Kay. He could not say anything meaningful until Em had given him some idea of what it was she wanted to talk about. He had his suspicions though...

'Hi Kay.' She did not sound her normal self. Her voice, normally so bright was now rendered in a distinctly minor key.

'How's things going?' Kay asked, waiting for her to broach the subject that had cost him all but a night's sleep.

'Kay, I... I...,' she trailed off to a halt, 'I just think there's something you should know'.

'And what's that?' His heart was beating at twice its normal rate.

'I... I won't be coming back. To the flat I mean'.

Kay tried to sound calm, 'Why's that darling?'.

There was a long pause, 'because something's happened'.

This was like drawing teeth, 'What, Em? Is there somebody else?'

There was a long, long pause, only a second or two but it seemed like a fortnight to Kay.

'Yes,' replied Em.

There was another pause as Kay took in the enormity of what he had just heard. Collecting his thoughts he said, 'Who is it Em? Anybody I know?'

This was clearly an easy question, 'No, just somebody I met on set'.

Despite an ocean of hurt, Kay collected his thoughts, 'Are you sure Em? I thought we had something special'.

'I know,' she replied and Kay could hear her weeping softly to herself. It was Em who now gathered herself together, 'We did Kay but… I don't know, it's so difficult to explain. Our outlook on life is just so different, it would never last'.

'Clearly having an unemployed insurance broker as a partner would no longer cut the mustard for a budding superstar,' thought Kay. He was hurt. Hurt and angry. Why had he ever trusted her?

'And your mind is quite made up?'

Another long, long pause.

'Yes'.

With this affirmative in his ears, Kay quietly terminated the call and put the phone down on the sofa beside him.

It was over.

PART 2

Chapter Twenty Four

Kay stood and gazed across the valley, past the river now flowing lazily towards its big brother the River Severn, then on to the Bristol Channel and ultimately the open ocean. He loved the times of change; the autumn when the browns, reds and golds were slowly retreating into the bleak greyness of winter and now in the Spring when those commonplace wayside trees, the hawthorn and the elder were bursting into luxuriant blossom. The river, this river, _his_ river had been a part of his life ever since he left the South East of England a little less than a decade ago. The change had been so dramatic that he referred to the period since then as his 'new' life although it was now scarcely that. The world had changed too, not for the better he told himself. And then there was Pia…

In the back of his mind, he knew had a choice to make, a choice which had the potential to render this new life of his a thing of the past too. Perhaps this time next year the river in its turn would be receding in his memory. It all rested on him and he had never felt so alone.

Still, it was a pleasant late spring afternoon with the odd cotton wool cloud drifting slowly across the sky, from time to time obscuring the sun and sending shadows flitting across the landscape. He turned and trudged back along the way he had come, his dog, Daniel, following obediently at his heels, down the muddy track that slowly widened until the point at which it became a small tarmacked lane and finally a fully-fledged road. The road led into the village and dropped him outside the little whitewashed cottage that had been his home for the last seven years.

On opening the door, he was greeted by the smaller of the two cats, a tabby female called Pixie. The other, a big black brute of a male, although without the necessary equipment to be called a proper tom was obviously out hunting. He rejoiced in the name of Henry and was the scourge of the local rodent population.

As a child Kay had been very fond of Kenneth Grahame's classic, *The Wind In The Willows* and now as a middle-aged man, he identified strongly with Ratty whom, he reflected wasn't a rat at all, but a water vole. Perhaps this was why he tended to feel sorry for Henry's luckless victims and would rescue them whenever possible. Most were, however, field or wood mice with the odd field or bank vole. In fact, he didn't know of even one occasion when Henry had caught a water vole but the risk was always there.

The front door opened directly onto the lounge. He kicked off his boots, put them on the rubber mat positioned just to the right of the door and headed towards the smaller door on the other side of the room that led to the kitchen. Here he removed his thin green jacket and switched on the kettle, returning to the lounge to open a window and play some music he had downloaded that morning. The sounds of *Dance Fever*, the new album from Florence and the Machine filled the small room.

Meanwhile the kettle had boiled and he silently returned to the kitchen to make a cup of tea. Henry came in through the cat flap and noisily demanded food even though it was a good two hours before his supper was due. Pixie, who was his littermate sat demurely on a kitchen chair, letting her brother do the lion's share of the agitation for whatever meal this was he was bellyaching for. Daniel, never one to pass up the chance of an impromptu snack joined Henry, making that pleading noise that dogs make when they suspect food is on its way.

To guarantee peace and quiet, Kay fed the animals and then set about getting his own belated lunch, a simple meal of bread and cheese, a couple of tomatoes followed by a banana and a KitKat. This would do him until he could be bothered to cook a meal in the evening. 'Cook' though was perhaps a misnomer. These days, the extent of his culinary exploits consisted of warming up ready meals from the supermarket in Monmouth. He hated himself for what he considered sheer laziness but he had no enthusiasm for cooking elaborate meals for just one.

In his early days in the village he would have walked the two hundred yards to The Drovers for a couple of pints before his dinner but the pub had shut during the covid pandemic of 2020-21 and the owners had shown no inclination to re-open despite vociferous protests from the villagers.

Still, today was the F.A. Cup Final between Liverpool and Chelsea and he wanted to ensure that his meagre meals would not interfere with his watching this on TV. A love of football was one of the few pleasures he had taken with him from his old life and he was looking forward to the game. The river at this point delineated the border between England and Wales where rugby very much ruled the roost and spread its tentacles well into Gloucestershire such that he was one of very few people in the village who would be watching the game this afternoon. He was not terribly interested in the build-up so ate his meal at the kitchen table whilst absent-mindedly attempting the crossword from that morning's newspaper. At four thirty he poured himself a beer and sat down in the armchair to watch the match.

Chapter Twenty Five

August – September 2012

For several days after his telephone conversation with Em, Kay seldom left the flat but stayed indoors downing the contents of their drinks cabinet trying to take his mind off of his loss. During this period he refused most calls on his mobile and did not reply to messages or texts (except one from his mother that he felt he really ought to respond to). Through the alcoholic fog, Kay tried to think out a strategy for breaking the news to his family and friends. In the end, he just sent out a uniform text to everyone which said, '*Just to let you know, Em and me no longer an item*'. He received in return a few messages of the '*sorry to hear that*' variety but fortunately nobody sought to interrogate him.

A few days later, Pat and Jim came round to collect her stuff. In truth, she didn't have much beyond lots of clothes and shoes and a couple of trips in Jim's latest car, a Sierra Cosworth, was sufficient.

The three of them had always got on well and once Kay had let them in, Pat hugged Kay and in an angry voice said, 'I'm sorry Kay, I just don't know what she's up to. Success must have gone to her head'.

'It's not your fault Pat, I guess it was inevitable once she hit the big time. She moves in different circles now, meets rich and powerful people'.

'But that doesn't excuse her treating you like this. Wait till I see her, I'll give her a piece of my mind. Stuck up little bitch!'

'Please try not to, she's young and obviously impressionable. I just hope she doesn't get too carried away with this celebrity thing'.

Pat shook her head. 'You were too good for her Kay. I don't know why you're defending her like this'.

Kay did not know why he was defending her either but he felt there was certainly something in his theory that outgrowing their partners was a characteristic of people who acquire success during the course of their lives, rather than are born into a family that takes it for granted. There were bigger things to sort out, such as her share of the car, but Em would have to deal with that for herself. In the event, she handed it all over to Joanne to deal with at arm's length and obviously paid through the nose for the privilege.

Another few days passed which coincided with the emptying of every bottle of booze in the house. Once this ritual had reached its logical conclusion, Kay felt more able to face the task of re-joining society. He had never suffered with a lack of willpower and realised that oblivion was not the answer. Nevertheless, the first thing he did was to call Raj to see if he fancied a beer.

Kay detected a note of sympathy in Raj's reply, 'Yes, of course, there's something I wanted to ask you anyway. When d'you fancy? I'm starting work in Manchester next Monday so it'll have to be this week'.

'How about tomorrow,' said Kay.

'Yeah fine, the Cittie of Yorke for a change? Seven o'clock?'

*

Uniquely in a London pub, the interior of the Cittie of Yorke contains a series of individual booths which make it ideal for intimate conversation. Fortunately, they found one of these unoccupied. When they had settled, Kay tried to explain to Raj the background to the break up of his relationship with Em but there really wasn't much to tell as far as his side of the story went. Simply, she'd gone to the Caribbean for three months and didn't come back. There was obviously more to her side of the story but Kay wasn't privy to that and so couldn't comment. But it helped immensely to pour his heart out to a friendly ear and Raj certainly provided that.

But Em wasn't the only topic of conversation, Raj had his own preoccupation, his forthcoming wedding. Despite their misgivings about his choosing a bride from a different culture, his family had finally endorsed the marriage and were looking forward to a big Indian, or at least a big partially Indian wedding.

'Er, you couldn't do me a favour could you mate?' asked Raj.

'Yes, what?' Kay replied somewhat suspiciously.

'You wouldn't um… be my best man would you? The job would normally go to a brother but I don't have any, so you're the next best thing… okay, that sounds like you're a last minute substitute but I don't mean it that way… Oh sod it, will you do the fucking thing?'

Kay laughed. 'Yes of course'.

'Phew! Thank Christ for that. I was afraid you'd tell me to fuck off'.

The conversation continued for another hour and another couple of pints. Just as he was about to leave, Raj said, 'by the way. Did you hear about G & B's offices?'

'No, what happened?'

'Apparently, soon after we left, they had to be fumigated. There was a real stink coming from Tony's room. In the end, after they'd had people crawling over every inch of the place, they found some wag had stuck a fish under his desk'.

'Couldn't happen to a nicer guy,' said Kay with a smirk.

'It was you, you bastard! Why can I never think of things like that? And yes you're right there's nobody deserved it more than him. What's more, it sounds like he's got a whole lot more shit heading his way. Jayne is apparently gathering evidence to press charges following their little meeting in the kitchen. Seems like she wasn't the only one; a whole load of women have put their hands up to be counted, going right back to the early days of G & B. D'you think they'll let us send him a food parcel when he goes down?'

'Yes, a cake with a rubber file in it,' laughed Kay.

It had been good to talk to Raj. The evening marked the beginning of his return to the land of the living and although he would have moments when he missed her intently, he could now see Em slowly receding in his rear-view mirror whilst he drove on to a new life, one that he hoped would be entirely different to that he was now leaving.

Chapter Twenty Six

September – December 2012

The following day, Kay phoned his old school-friend Paul. The main purpose of the call was to establish how easy it would be to nail down a job working in the environment and with wildlife.

Paul's response was that with perseverance and a willingness to move to the work, it ought to be possible but the pay would most likely be at or near minimum wage and long-term he really ought to try and get some exams behind him. Paul wished him luck.

A couple of days later, Paul phoned back. There was a short term job on offer providing maternity cover in Cornwall and working directly with him. Would Kay like to apply?

'I'll have to find somewhere to live,' replied Kay.

'That shouldn't be a problem, I have a friend who rents out what amount to bedsits or 'studio flats' as they now call them and off-season they shouldn't be that dear. If you're interested I'll have a word.'

So it was that Kay found himself living in Truro and working at any number of locations in the county of Cornwall. The job was extremely hard physical work compared with what he was used to and to start off with he found himself returning to his tiny flat completely exhausted. He had to remind himself that what he was actually doing was maternity cover which meant that the week before he started, a pregnant woman had been doing the job. Coming from the macho world of finance, this gave him pause for thought…

The job mostly consisted of maintaining and erecting nesting boxes for all manner of birds as well as bats and mice. Some of these boxes were at a considerable height which initially caused him some issues as he had never liked climbing ladders. But if he was to succeed in this new role, it was certainly something he would need to get used to.

Other than that, he would often find himself detailed to undertake reserve maintenance which could involve such tasks as cutting scrub with a brush cutter, trimming bushes, occasionally felling trees or repairing fences. He had felt towards the end of his time at G & B that he was beginning to get a bit soft but this job was the complete antidote to that. After a few months he had become, in relative terms, fit and lean.

Paul could be a hard taskmaster but unlike Tony, you knew where you stood with him and he was always prepared to chew the fat after work with honesty and good humour. The tradition of retiring to a pub for a couple of pints after work pre-dated Kay who was allowed to slot seamlessly into these informal de-briefing sessions. In attendance were usually two or three professionals in addition to Paul and Kay, as well as a variable number of volunteers who would usually work one day or perhaps even only half a day a week. This meant that there was a constant stream of new names and faces as well as details of their partners and home lives to be memorised.

One of these volunteers was called Rachel, an energetic and forthright divorcee in her early forties. At first, Kay found her somewhat overpowering but she had slowly grown on him. A little while after this stage had been reached, they became lovers in the sense that they would occasionally share a bed. It was ultimately one of those unsatisfactory, on-off, going nowhere relationships that kill time, satisfy carnal desires but precious little else. Their interactions were limited to sex and the odd shared drink but Kay didn't feel he was using Rachel any more than Rachel was using him. Kay knew she had at least one other lover but that did not bother him. They were both just waiting for someone more suitable to come along and in the meantime the relationship fulfilled a mutual need. When it was over, as inevitably it would be, they could continue to correspond in a desultory way as friends, with no feelings of rancour on either side.

*

Kay spent that Christmas at his parents' house in Amersham. The journey back from Truro was painfully slow and ultimately took over eight hours, a consequence of having to travel on the last Saturday before Christmas which was on a Monday this year. He had bought out Em's share in the Alfa and whilst it could at times seem out of place in Cornwall, long journeys like this put it much more in its comfort zone.

Christmas was pleasant but with Jack a teenager and all that entailed, it lacked some of the magic of previous years. This was reflected on Christmas Day itself with Kay retiring to bed well before midnight. He was sleeping in his old room with its memories of his own youth. It looked almost as it had that autumn when he had left for university. Even some of his old posters were on the wall - Guns N' Roses, Courtney Love, as well as a photograph of a fox he had taken in the garden circa 1994. It all combined to give a feeling of timelessness but lying here alone at the age of thirty five, it also projected a sense of failure. He had spent too long in a career that clearly was not for him and his two attempts at long term relationships had ended without successful conclusions.

It was at times like this that he missed Em the most. He allowed himself to think about her at length. What was she doing now? Was there even a small part of her that missed him? He answered his own questions; she was all tied up in a film star lifestyle and that was what she had wanted from day one. He was just a stepping stone on the way to fame and fortune, something to be used and then ignored as if it had never existed. Sometimes his anger overwhelmed him. He had supported her completely, helping her to prepare for parts that turned out to be great successes, supported her financially in the early days. And for what? To be simply tossed aside like a baker would discard yesterday's stale loaf.

There was a part of him that didn't entirely believe this narrative. He thought he had seen evidence of considerable humility in her. She wasn't arrogant or even particularly self-centred, so what had happened? He obviously didn't have the evidence to answer this question which frustrated him immensely. Eventually, he fell asleep only to be haunted by the same dream as that night before their fateful telephone conversation where Em drifted just out of reach before disappearing entirely from view.

Although he didn't want to admit it to himself, he was glad to be returning to Cornwall despite the virtual inevitability of traffic jams en route. His family had been good to him but other than that, there was no longer much to keep him in the South East, his friends had mostly settled down and moved away. Besides, his new career had given him a sense of vocation and for the first time in his life, he had begun to feel that what he did during the daylight hours was actually important. In the great scheme of things, it never made a fig of difference whether his clients bought insurance from him or from somebody else but somehow he now felt a personal responsibility for the wildlife of the South West and he couldn't wait to get back to them.

Chapter Twenty Seven

Spring 2013

One day in early spring, Paul called Kay's mobile.

'I've got a job for you.'

In his previous life, had Tony or Mike uttered these words, Kay's heart would have sunk. It would usually have been along the lines of contacting some awkward client who was complaining that due to the incompetence of Gresham & Bailey, his policy had lapsed and he was currently uninsured. But that was a world away. There *were* unpleasant tasks, such as removing the corpse of a badger from a footpath running through a reserve or raking blanket weed from a pond but these were as nothing compared with the hospital pass that Tony Bailey could have thrown him on a bad day. Besides, there was something in Paul's voice that didn't indicate a particularly unpleasant task.

'Okay, what is it?'

'I just got a phone call from BBC Radio Cornwall. Next Thursday, they want somebody to be interviewed on the possible reintroduction of beavers to the South West. I can't do it as I'm in the Scillies all day. Can you mug up on it and take it on? I warn you, nobody else was that that keen'.

'That's something different. Yeah okay, I'm always up for a challenge'.

Kay, of course, knew that the thing was a *fait accompli* anyway. For the last five years beavers had been quite happily living in the River Otter in East Devon. Nobody knew, or at least nobody would admit to knowing, how they had got there. It was unthinkable that they could be removed at this late stage. Moreover, trial reintroductions were already underway in Scotland and word was that they were going well.

So, on Thursday April 4th, Kay turned up at the studios of BBC Radio Cornwall, which as it happened was only a short walk from his flat. He knew that he had been lined up to present the 'pro' arguments whilst opposing him, a local landowner was in the 'anti' camp.

The discussion was only scheduled to last for five minutes and when it was over, Kay felt that it had gone pretty well. The arguments he had put across that, albeit four hundred years ago, beavers should never have been removed from the countryside in the first place and that they had a role to play in flood prevention seemed to him to be quite persuasive.

In a sense, as only a few thousand people were likely to be listening, its impact was probably close to zero but that day, Kay believed he had struck a blow for the conservation movement in general.

When he got back to work, Paul telephoned him to congratulate him on his performance.

'That went really well Kay, you seem to have a gift for speaking. I'll have to buy you an extra pint tomorrow.'

In fact it had gone so well that in the next few months, Kay was twice more called in to speak on local radio as well as giving a talk at the Bodmin Women's Institute entitled '*The Return of the Cornish Chough*'.

*

While he was heavily engaged at work, he seldom thought of Em but in the evenings when he was on his own, he thought of her often. At first he actively tried to avoid anything in the media relating to her career but sometimes he would have needed to be a hermit to miss it. *The Plantation* had been a colossal success, so much so that there was some suggestion that the film would be nominated for an Academy Award. Whilst this did not materialise, it nonetheless earned the film company and its distributors an enormous profit.

Ever since *The Plantation,* the tabloid press had taken a keen interest in Em's life and it was from a discarded newspaper lying outside W.H. Smith's in Falmouth that he learnt she had for some months been living with Monty McLay. The paper also claimed to have been informed by 'a friend' that their marriage was imminent. For a moment Kay regretted that he had not asked her to marry him but what good would that have done? She would inevitably have gone her own way and it would just have massively complicated the painful task of disentangling their lives. The newspaper report did, however, clear up one mystery; the 'somebody she met on set' was none other than the great director himself.

His curiosity had now been piqued, so as soon as he got home Kay googled Monty McLay. According to Wikipedia, he came from a wealthy landowning family linked to the Earls of Caithness, with an estate in the Scottish Borders. Although only a year older than Kay, he had already been married and divorced twice. Digging further, Kay discovered that he now lived in, or at least owned, a faux Palladian mansion in Gerrards Cross, well-known as being reputedly the most expensive town anywhere in the country and barely a stone's throw from Pinewood Studios. His neighbours there included bankers, pop stars, chairmen of large public companies and the odd Russian oligarch.

So this was the new world into which Em had parachuted. Frankly, short of marrying into royalty she could not have landed higher up the social scale. He could picture her dressed head to toe in Gucci, driving her Lamborghini to the exclusive tennis club to play a couple of sets with a countess or an Austrian princess. This was way above even footballers' wives territory. He wondered if Pat and Jim still lived on the Old Oak Common Estate…

*

Raj and Kate's wedding was scheduled for April 20th in Colchester, a long and difficult journey from Cornwall. As the stag do was in London on the Wednesday before the wedding, Kay decided to travel from Cornwall on the Tuesday, spend the night in Amersham and then catch the train down to London and check in at the inevitable Premier Inn on Wednesday afternoon.

Despite the occasion, Kay's week was tinged with sadness as his mother had telephoned him the previous night to say that his grandfather was going downhill rapidly. Given that he would be in the area, Kay obviously wanted to take the opportunity to drop in and see him before they all had to bow to the inevitable. The journey thus far had been relatively uneventful giving him plenty of time to call in at the retirement home on Tuesday afternoon.

With his heavily accented English, Kay had often found his grandfather hard to understand but now his dementia made it all but impossible. This was hard for Kay to take as he was very fond of the old man and childhood memories of sunny days playing in his grandparents' garden in Ealing or sitting on his grandfather's knee whilst he was read a story continually came to mind. There was nothing more Kay could do other than just sit there and hold the old man's cold, grey hand while he mumbled incoherently. Although it was clear that he was virtually unaware of his presence, Kay stayed in the home for over two hours and left just as the clock in reception struck five.

His time in London was a bit of a blur but it was obvious that they had all got horribly drunk and Kay did not wake up until an impatient maid knocked loudly on his bedroom door at eleven o'clock enquiring as to when he was going to stir himself as she wanted to clean the room. He quickly cleared up and caught the Metropolitan Line back towards Amersham without even attempting to take breakfast. Although he had the rest of the day to kill, he actually did nothing of note other than hang around in his parents' lounge watching daytime TV, drinking coffee and eating biscuits, a rare treat given his current full-on lifestyle. The following morning, he left Amersham at midday and made his way round the M25 towards Colchester, arriving shortly before two.

The wedding venue displayed the usual sort of chaos associated with such places the day before an event was due to take place. Kay attempted, largely ineffectually to lend a hand but realising that he was being more of a hindrance than a help, retired to his hotel for dinner and a couple of glasses of Merlot before turning in at nine thirty.

Over the previous three weeks, he had diligently put together a best man's speech full of coarse humour and ribaldry but then, not being sure how it would be taken by some of the older relatives attending, tore it up, wrote a much milder version and then wished he hadn't. In the end, what emerged was a meld of the two and other than an elderly aunt of Raj's who sat po-faced through the whole performance, nobody seemed to be offended. It was later pointed out to Kay that the elderly aunt spoke not a word of English and was in any event as deaf as a post.

The wedding went better than expected considering that during the excesses of Wednesday night, the groom's face and a portion of pavement in Leicester Square had become more closely acquainted than was strictly necessary, leaving a large graze on his forehead. Kate was incandescent and blamed everything under the sun, including Kay, for this less than ideal state of affairs. Fortunately, by the morning of the wedding she had calmed down and if you looked at Raj in certain lights you didn't notice the graze anyway.

Jayne and Dan had both been invited and once the formalities were over, Kay took the opportunity to ask Jayne how her action against Tony was progressing.

'Sam Mepham has put me in touch with four other women who claim they were sexually assaulted by Tony Bailey and I'm still trying to track down another. His millions aren't going to save him, he's going down for a good long stretch,' Jayne told him triumphantly.

Being one of very few unattached males at the wedding, Kay could have had the pick of the women there in a similar position but none of them appealed particularly and despite lengthy dances with several women, including Raj's sister, he rolled into bed alone at half past one.

*

First thing next morning, Kay received a text from his mother the thrust of which was to say that his grandfather was unlikely to survive more than a few hours and asking if he could get home as soon as possible. By the time he got to Amersham however, it was too late, old Manny had already passed away. Despite his grandfather's age and infirmity, Kay was immediately struck with a profound sense of loss. He had not seen the old man very much in recent years and this fact alone, filled him with guilt as well as grief.

Unsurprisingly, Manny had seldom spoken about his experiences during the war but in his late sixties he had made a trip back to Berlin to re-live some of the events of his youth and to belatedly mourn the overwhelming majority of his family who had not survived the gas chambers. The experience of being in the environment in which he was brought up, although much changed, completely overwhelmed him and at the last minute he cancelled a planned trip to Auschwitz.

In the last few years of his life, he had taken tentative steps to make his peace with the religion of his birth and could sometimes be seen at the Ealing Liberal Synagogue whenever he could persuade another elderly Jew to give him a lift. Although not the strict conservative religion in which he was raised, this freer form of Judaism seemed to give him a connection to his ancestors without having to adhere to the full strictures of orthodoxy. It was for this reason that the family decided to give him a Jewish funeral in Willesden. Although they were not able to bury him within the traditional twenty four hours after death, the funeral was arranged for the following Thursday, a considerably shorter time than has become the general norm in England.

As he had few living relatives, the occasion was largely restricted to his descendants, their partners and friends, few of whom were actually Jewish. But for the first time in his life, Kay wore a kippah for the funeral and was quite proud to do so. This one act seemed to give him a sense of belonging and he felt it brought him closer to his late grandfather and the Jewish tradition in which he had been raised.

Chapter Twenty Eight

September 2013 - March 2014

Kay's time in Cornwall was coming to an end. The woman for whom he was providing maternity cover was due to return to work in September and had signalled her willingness to return. Paul had fought hard to retain him on the payroll but the money was just not there, so he had to move on.

Given his level of experience, particularly when it came to his willingness to speak to the media, Paul expressed his opinion that it would not be at all difficult for Kay to find another job in the sector and promised to alert all his contacts in the wildlife trusts, RSPB, National Trust etcetera.

As it happened, it was rather more difficult than Paul had anticipated. Most potential employers seemed to want a degree in Environmental Science or similar. Kay had already started a degree course in just this subject at the Open University but this did not seem to be enough. Eventually however, he was offered a position as a reserve officer with something of a roving brief, largely centred around an expansive nature reserve sandwiched between the Welsh border and the Forest of Dean. Again, the money was not great but as he had built up considerable savings during his time at G & B, he was not going to go hungry. Added to this, he was likely to inherit an as yet unknown sum from his grandfather's estate, so he felt that for the time being at least, he would be able to cope with a fairly meagre income.

Obviously, the first thing he needed to do was to fix up somewhere to live and after a brief period of searching, eventually settled on a small flat over a shop in Coleford that was reasonably handy for work.

The work was actually quite similar to what he had been doing in Cornwall but the rolling countryside was much more wooded, with the fields lying between the sylvan hilltops being laid mainly to grass. It was now Autumn, the leaves were turning and there was a distinct chill in the air that meant Winter was not far away. Reserve maintenance during the colder months was a distinct downside to the job but as anyone who works outdoors knows, if approached with a degree of vigour, the cold weather can be kept at bay.

Despite the icy days and long nights, Kay was beginning to take to the area with its sparse population and spectacular views. One Sunday he went to Symonds Yat, perhaps one of the finest vistas in England and stayed for over an hour just staring down at the River Wye as it flowed through the tight limestone gorge. He remembered reading that both peregrines and goshawks could be seen here but this day he saw neither. In the fullness of time however, he would see both in increasing numbers but he never ceased to be thrilled when a peregrine flew at great pace overhead or a goshawk broke cover chasing a hapless pigeon.

In his first week, the trust sent him on a First Aid course, considered essential for outdoor workers. It was held in a large meeting room with walls covered in photographs depicting many of the species of fauna that could be seen in the lower Wye valley, everything from merlins through polecats to adders and common frogs. Most of the others attending were obviously work colleagues and Kay was introduced to them one by one. Including him, there were ten attendees, an equal split between men and women. Among the latter, Kay's attention was drawn to a striking woman with long wavy hair mid-way between auburn and ginger in colour. Her complexion was ruddy and her hands somewhat gnarled, both no doubt indicating a life spent largely outdoors. Kay assessed her as being roughly his own age and for some reason, his mind conjured up Raj describing her as 'fit as a butcher's dog'.

Most of us make assumptions about individuals based on their given names. Some like James, Sarah, Rachel or George however, are largely ubiquitous and do not say much about their owners. Hermione, Rupert, Cecil or Camilla however, summon up broadly similar images in maybe 95% of us. So, it was with some sense of incongruity that Kay learned her name was Pia. When he had heard the name before, which was very, very rarely, he would immediately think of somebody slight, perhaps olive-skinned in line with the name's Latin origins, working in maybe a library or a solicitor's office. What he would not think of was a healthy looking, ruddy-faced Englishwoman dressed all in green, and smoking (as he soon found out) liquorice paper roll-ups.

And he had heard the name quite recently too. Wasn't Pia the name of the woman who had inspired Paul to opt for a life among the birds and the forests? Given the name's scarcity, was it likely that there would be two people called Pia working in wildlife conservation in the United Kingdom?

Kay thought he would test the theory. After they had been introduced he ventured, 'I hope you don't mind me saying but I think I might know an old friend of yours.'

'Go on, who?' Pia replied, clearly interested in what Kay had to say.

'Okay, do you know Paul Maisey?'

'Ha, ha Paul! Yes, we go back a long way. Old Tiger Maisey. I can't have seen him for ten years or more. How is the old git?'

'Fine, he's now a director of a wildlife trust in the West Country. Wife and young kid with another on the way.'

'Glad he's doing well. Give him my love when you speak to him,' Pia replied. 'Well, well, Paul Maisey,' she repeated shaking her head.

'He was very complimentary about you. Said it was you that inspired him to make a career in wildlife.'

'Paul was a nice lad. We had a bit of a thing going for a while but we were both young and I think it all ended after I took a job on the Isle of Lewis. It's a bit difficult to keep any relationship going when you're five hundred miles and a stretch of cold water apart'.

Pia had the kind of voice that suggested somebody who knew what they wanted out of life. It was clear, insistent and enthusiastic. Kay could well believe that she would inspire a young man to follow a particular path in life.

After the course had started, the first aid instructor split up the attendees into pairs to demonstrate various aspects of artificial respiration. As luck would have it, Kay was coupled with Pia and although touching was clearly forbidden, they spent the entire two and a half hours in close proximity to one other.

Pia's job was similar to Kay's although she was clearly his superior, having management responsibilities in addition to a more hands-on role, in her case mainly in the Forest of Dean. Their paths would cross several times in the next few weeks, both professionally and in the informal after work sessions which were just as much a feature here as they had been in Cornwall. It did not surprise Kay that Pia's drink of choice was one of several local ciders, the coarser and drier the better. These she drank in pints, never halves, although to be fair to her she was frequently driving and on these occasions she would have a pint, no more, of a low gravity local ale.

Kay also soon learnt that she was recently divorced, having married a stir-crazy Scotsman during her sojourn in the Hebrides. The marriage had been a disaster from start to finish and did not actually last much more than a year before they had gone their separate ways. Neither of them however, was in any great rush to formally end the arrangement and so it had taken until the beginning of the current year for the divorce to be finalised. After she had left her husband there had followed two further co-habitations, both in Gloucestershire but neither of these were even close to resulting in a more permanent arrangement.

It took Kay nearly three and a half months of knowing Pia before he made the suggestion that they might like to have a meal together. This was not hesitance on his part, merely that the idea had not occurred to him before. And it was not that he didn't find her attractive, he did, but they had become friends and confidantes first and in a sense that made it all the more difficult. Nonetheless, by the early spring he was seldom sleeping alone.

Chapter Twenty Nine

Kay's relationship with Em was now some way in the past and his initial reluctance to follow her career had abated. Following her, or at least reports of her was not a difficult thing to do - the tabloids were constantly reporting her movements. From the *Mirror* he learnt that she had indeed married Monty McLay, co-incidentally on the same weekend that Raj had married Kate. Reflecting her new lifestyle, the event had taken place in Martinique with pop and film stars and even minor royalty in attendance. Kay sighed, he could never in a million years have kept pace with this, it was so far out of his league as to be on another planet.

Historical dramas were Monty McLay's 'thing' and the filming of another historical drama was now taking place, this time based on the Trojan Wars. To be called simply *'Helen'* it starred his new wife in the title role as Helen of Troy and was likely to be premiered early next year.

Monty and Em were the sought after celebrity couple of the moment, almost the new Posh and Becks. Women's magazines which Kay read online when no-one was looking, would sometimes have interviews with either the pair of them (which must have cost a fortune) or with Em alone. Never did she make any mention of him and again this touched a raw nerve. None of this would he admit to anybody in his new life, least of all Pia. Even though he confided in her on most things, this area of his life was strictly under wraps.

That June, he cut one of his last links with Em. The Alfa Romeo, which his colleagues in Gloucestershire called with a distinct lack of originality, his 'Hairdresser's Car' was swapped for a thoroughly disreputable Land Rover, almost as old as him. Given his green credentials, he would have liked a fully electric car but right at this moment, that was neither affordable nor practical. Nonetheless, the Land Rover gave him a sense of belonging, it completed his membership application to the club representing that small minority of people who both live and work in the country.

It would be easy though to make the mistake of assuming that Kay had arrived in some form of bucolic idyll. He had a good rapport with his colleagues and those generally who worked in conservation. But there were some flies in the ointment. Most farmers and people who worked on the land were absolutely fine and could see the benefit of what the conservationists were doing. But it was undeniable that there were others, admittedly few in number, who wanted a return to the old countryside ways of shooting, trapping or hunting down anything that moved. There were also a tiny number of farmers who insisted on following the profit motive to the absolute exclusion of everything else. These took the view that much of the legislation aimed at the conservation of wildlife and habitat that had been passed over the previous twenty years or more did not apply to them.

It was well known among the conservationists that there was a shooting estate to the north of the county where any raptor, or indeed anybody bent on their protection, entered very much at their peril. Pia always found it hard to disguise her views and had told Kay of the occasion when she had had a heated discussion in a pub, not a million miles from this estate, concerning the persecution of raptors. None of the people she was arguing with were known to her but three days later she got up to find that in the dead of night someone had dropped the corpse of a young peregrine, full of shot on her doorstep. Through her door had been posted a note torn out of an exercise book, which said in block capitals, 'YOU NEXT'. She told the police but where she lived was far away from the nearest CCTV camera and unsurprisingly they informed her that they would hold the incident on file but there was really very little they could do without a suspect.

*

Pia never ceased to surprise Kay. Some while after they had met, she revealed to him that her late father had been a baronet. Sir Rodney Sinclair Standish, Bt. had lived and several times almost died for his hobby of shooting. He would shoot almost anything that both moved or flew – pheasant, partridge, snipe, woodcock and when they weren't available, pigeons, any form of wildfowl, and a whole lot of creatures besides, that he was not actually supposed to shoot. The highlight of his year was the Glorious Twelfth of August, a few days before which he would pack up his venerable Volvo, technically an Estate but he insisted on calling it his 'Shooting-Brake', and head for Scotland via a small estate near Penrith that was owned by an old chum from his schooldays at Winchester.

Pia's mother Sandra, by way of contrast, was from much humbler stock. She had been born and brought up on a council estate in Maidstone and after winning a talent contest, removed to London to become, amongst other things, a dancer in any number of West End shows. It was after one of these that a friend introduced her to Rodney. At that time he was a handsome Lieutenant in the Grenadier Guards and heir to what appeared to be half of Northamptonshire. The relationship did not last long, just long enough for Sandra to become pregnant with Pia.

This was something of a problem for the young aristocrat but doubtless one faced by several of his esteemed ancestors. He would actually become the 10th Baronet, the first having been a minor official in Sir Robert Walpole's Administration. His progenitor's special talent according to his pals at Winchester was the wiping of the royal bottom, in this instance that of King George II. This particular gentleness of touch allowed the eldest male descendant of every succeeding generation to call himself by the title 'Sir' without actually having done anything to deserve the accolade beyond possessing the ability to choose his father wisely.

Rodney's father, the 9th Baronet insisted that he pay Sandra off handsomely to purchase her silence, and have nothing more to do with her. This he did with one exception, he requested, in fact it was closer to a demand, that the girl be educated at his mother's *alma mater*, Flintcombe Abbey School, one of the most expensive girls' public schools in the country.

This was not the master stroke that Rodney (Sir Rodney from just after Pia's eleventh birthday) had thought it would be. The girl, who for anonymity's sake was given her mother's surname of Cutbush, proved to be a natural rebel, constantly breaking rules and at some point absconding from school every year, until at the age of fifteen, the school insisted that their reputation was at stake and Pia had to go.

The final straw that broke the camel's back was Pia being caught *in flagrante delicto* in a disused dormitory with a boy (the headmistress called him a 'ruffian') from the town. What made it worse was that Pia failed to accept that she had done anything wrong and actually had the temerity to say she had enjoyed the little encounter.

Following this episode, Pia went to live with her mother in Tooting where she had spent most of the holidays anyway. Although she would hang around street corners smoking dope and generally getting into scrapes, Pia had a good deal of affection for her mother and tried with, it has to be said, limited success to shield her from some of the more outrageous behaviour to which she was prone. Seeing that Sandra was at her wit's end, Pia's maternal grandmother opined that what she needed was a focus in life. After several false starts Pia ultimately found this by vehemently opposing everything for which her absent father stood.

By her sixteenth birthday, she had become a vegan, had three times been arrested on environmental protest marches, had glued herself to the railings outside Downing Street and a short while later was again arrested, this time for hitting a Conservative MP in the eye with an egg thrown from no more than two metres away.

With all this behind her, it was with incredulity that her family received the news that she had got a job, and one that suited her too. She was to be a junior in the Countryside Department of Kent County Council. The location of the job meant that she had to live with her grandmother five days of the week but that was no great hardship. The post calmed her down markedly but not before she had been arrested yet again for attempting to knock a policeman's helmet off at another protest march. A year later she moved to work with the National Trust in Sussex which was where she met and inspired Paul.

Chapter Thirty

Spring 2014 – Spring 2015

Kay received the portion of his grandfather's estate allotted to
him in the Spring following his move to Gloucestershire. Manny
had worked hard after his arrival in England. His father back in
Germany had been a wine merchant but he had been too young
to learn anything about the business before it was all wiped away
in the Holocaust. Hence, when he came to England, he was not
possessed of any trade and had to learn one from scratch. So, as
soon as he left the Lake District, he obtained cheap lodgings
from a sympathetic family in Acton and took up an engineering
apprenticeship with Napier Aero Engines just a few hundred
yards away in Acton Vale.

He figured he was the only Jewish engineer in the company
but he got on well with his colleagues and his capacity for hard
work commended him to his bosses, such that his career
progression was far quicker than he could have hoped. The
Napier factory closed in 1963 but his services were immediately
sought by Lucas CAV, just around the corner in Warple Way.
He eventually became a freelance engineer and retired in 1992
having made a good living for himself, and by extension his

family. This meant that once his estate had been determined, each of his seven grandchildren received just over £120,000.

Kay had obviously got an inkling of how much his inheritance would be and now that he was settled in his work, he determined to put it into property. The part of rural Gloucestershire in which he now found himself was some way from being the most expensive area in the country and although he could not expect to buy a property outright, this amount ought to be sufficient to at least get him on the first rung of the ladder.

The house he eventually settled on was a small terraced cottage in the village of Ivywell, nestling in a fold of the hills just above the Wye. The cottage dated from the late 18th century and would need some re-commissioning, having been the home of an elderly widow who had died more than a year earlier. The idea was not necessarily for Pia to live with him, she had her own place in Cinderford on the east side of the forest but she was welcome to stay there whenever the mood took her.

Kay moved into the cottage that Autumn and he and Pia spent several months re-decorating his new home, ridding the small garden of weeds and arranging for the fitting of various kitchen appliances. This work took him well into the New Year but by March it was virtually complete or complete in as much as any work on a house can ever be said to be truly finished.

As it happened, Pia spent most of her nights there. She had recently acquired a springer spaniel puppy and two kittens. Given that she was at his cottage more often than not and despite his misgivings, the kittens moved in permanently with Kay, while the puppy, which she called Daniel (to rhyme with spaniel), came to work with Pia and went virtually everywhere she went.

Other than a couple of short lived hamsters when he was a child, Kay had never had to look after pets before and the responsibility troubled him. How much food should he give them? Why do they never seem to drink much? Should he really be letting them climb up the curtains? As time went by however, the cats became part of the fabric of the place and he could not imagine the cottage without them, but he did have a tendency to worry about them, particularly if they were outside the cottage for longer than expected.

*

It seemed that one of the reasons the wildlife trust had employed Kay in the first place was because of his experience with the media. Once he had settled in and begun to learn more detail concerning the fauna of the area, the local radio interviews started up again. Within a short period of time, he gave interviews on subjects including shrews, adders, nightingales and then an old favourite, beavers. All the time, he was growing in confidence and after a while was told by the Chief Executive that the radio station would now ask for him by name when planning their wildlife output. It was suggested to him that he might like to make this a much more formal part of his role but this would have meant spending more time in the office and he turned it down. Having expended most of his working life in offices, he felt that it was just too soon to return to a life largely spent behind a computer screen.

Another skill that he was beginning to acquire was that of sketching and sometimes painting the wildlife he would encounter in his everyday life. He spent hours practising drawing birds, animals, insects, amphibians and so on. He kept a pad in the cottage for when the spirit moved him. It was very much a mood thing. Sometimes he would draw every day, other times not for weeks but by the time he had lived in Gloucestershire for eighteen months he was beginning to build up a substantial body of work. Pia was admiring of his drawings and when he asked her to name her favourite, she immediately picked one out. It was of a small tortoiseshell.

Chapter Thirty One

Summer 2015

Following their departure from London and subsequent marriage, Raj and Kate had bought a large Victorian house in Ashton-under-Lyne and a year after their marriage, a daughter whom they called Sita arrived. Although they had been living together for a total of eight years, the fact that the child was born more than nine months after their marriage seemed to mean a lot to Raj's parents.

Although Kay had told Raj all about Pia, they had never actually met. To remedy this situation, that June, Kay invited him and Kate to stay with them for a long weekend. They kept in touch frequently by phone but it was never the same as meeting up in the flesh. At one hundred and sixty odd miles and a nearly three hour journey each way, it was a long trip with a toddler. For her part, Pia had never met any of Kay's friends from his old life and indeed was still to meet his parents. It would therefore be a learning experience for her too.

On the day of their visit, the weather forecast was for warm and sunny weather with the outside chance of a shower in the afternoon. Ninety nine percent of the time Pia would wear nothing more formal than shorts or jeans and a tee-shirt but that morning when she came downstairs she was wearing a long white dress that clung to her sensuously.

'Bloomin' 'eck,' said Kay resorting to a cockney accent which he had never actually been born to.

'Something wrong?'

'Do we have sex now or later? You look...,' he thought for a moment but failing to come up with the right word just said, 'Wow!'

'Sadly my sweet boy, I fear it will have to be later. Your friends are due here soon and I would rather not have stains on my nice clean frock when they get here'.

Raj and Kate arrived just before one o'clock in a brand new Audi so he was obviously doing well. It was clear though that Sita had had enough of the journey and was letting her feelings be known by screaming at the top of her voice. When she caught sight of Daniel however, she calmed down and pointing a small chubby finger said' 'doggy' and held out her arms as if she wanted to hold him. Fortunately, Daniel had a very placid nature and allowed himself to be pulled around, under the close supervision of his parents of course. When Sita caught sight of Pixie she was in heaven and her wailing of just a few minutes ago was completely forgotten. Kay knitted his brow, Pixie would be fine but he was not sure how Henry would react.

Kay introduced Pia to his friends and was quite surprised that Pia was happy to hold and play with the child. Somehow, he just had not seen her as the maternal type, but clearly he was wrong. In fact this came back to bite her over lunch as Sita managed to grab a handful of her dress while she was leaning over talking baby language to the child. The hand proved to be full of baby

190

food and so Pia had to return upstairs and change into her more customary shorts and tee-shirt.

'The job is fine,' said Raj in response to Kay's enquiry as to how he was coping at Legal & Provincial in the centre of Manchester, 'but it's a big company. There's so many rules and so little flexibility that it can drive you nuts at times. At least at Gresham & Bailey we had a healthy disregard for rules...'.

'Except for Tony,' interrupted Kay, 'he had a distinctly unhealthy disregard for rules'.

'Which reminds me,' said Raj, 'I spoke to Jayne last week.'

'Great. How's she getting on?'.

'Job wise, fine. She's a legal executive now for a firm of solicitors in Richmond. But her action against Tony seems to have run into the sand'.

'So what happened?'

'Well, it was like this. Jayne and the other women had everything together to make a case against him. The DPP were willing but then all of a sudden he disappeared. The rumour is that he caught a one way flight to Bangkok and that was the last anyone heard of him'.

'I bet Jayne was sick'.

'They all were. It had been ten, twelve years for some of them and he just buggers off to Thailand'.

When the two men were alone, Raj shook his head and said, 'You've done it again. You've pulled another cracker'.

'A very different one to the last time,' replied Kay. 'She's more my age. Perhaps I'm getting old but I rather like that'.

In fact when Kay had estimated that she was about the same age as him, he had been more accurate than he realised. She was in fact his elder by six days, her birthday being on May 28th and his on June 3rd .

'She's actually one tough cookie,' continued Kay, 'you seriously would not want to get on the wrong side of her. One thing I've noticed though that I didn't realise until you came here with Sita – she actually has a maternal streak. I hadn't expected that'.

When they were all together again, Kay made a suggestion, 'Come on, let me show you the village'. Kate put Sita in her push chair and they set off, Kay and Pia acting as tour guides, being towed along by an eager Daniel whilst pointing out small vernacular cottages where this or the other trade was practised, the village pub, the Norman church, the best view across the Wye and so on. On their way back they dropped into the garden of The Drovers and had a relaxing drink whilst Sita tottered around, frequently collapsing in a heap on the ground and being picked up by any one of them.

On the way home the heavens opened and they all, with the exception of Sita, who had a little plastic canopy over her buggy, got drenched. By the time they got back to the cottage however, the clouds had passed and it was sunny again.

The previous month there had been a General Election and that evening they spent much of their time arguing, in a very friendly way, about the result. Pia was the most strident in her disappointment. The environment was everything to her and she was worried that the new administration, although it was not hugely different from the last would backslide on its international environmental commitments in the same way as the United States had following the 1997 Kyoto Accord. On the other hand, Raj was broadly happy with the result which was in stark contrast to Kate who said she would not trust David Cameron further than she could throw him. The argument blew itself out at about ten o'clock and they finished the evening playing Dingbats; Kate and Pia against Raj and Kay with the latter winning by the narrow margin of three points.

The following morning, they all went up to Symonds Yat to see the spectacular views across the river and the countryside beyond. They followed this up with a short boat ride on the river and had the good fortune to see a kingfisher darting along the river bank. Although such sights were now commonplace to Pia and Kay and not entirely unknown to Kate from her upbringing on the Essex/Suffolk borders, it was the first time that Raj, the city boy, had seen one. 'Wow, isn't it bright!' he exclaimed as the bird disappeared among the willows. Because they had Sita and Daniel in tow, they considered it unwise to eat inside the pub but opted to have their lunch under the canopy outside the Saracen's Head which stands little more than the width of a narrow lane from the river.

Kate and Raj could not stay much beyond late afternoon and left just as the clock struck four. The weekend had been a success and it was clear to Kay that Pia had made a great impression on his friends. He was glad about this because he knew she had made a huge impact on him. More perhaps than she would ever know.

Chapter Thirty Two

Every few weeks, Pia would drive to South London to see her mother. Since Pia's birth, she had been married and divorced, then married again and was now separated from her second husband. Having reached her late fifties, she now lived in a pleasant terraced house in Tooting with Pia's twenty two year old half-brother, Christopher.

Somewhat reluctantly Pia and Kay decided that he would accompany her on her next visit and if they timed it right they could drop in and see his parents on the way. Land Rovers are not the ideal vehicle for motorway travel and they therefore opted for Pia's almost as ancient Polo. Making a fairly early start they arrived in Amersham just before twelve, in good time for lunch.

Pia was the third serious girlfriend that Kay had presented to his parents. There was studious Vicky, ambitious Em but what epithet would they apply to the woman sitting in front of them now? Forthright? Committed? Resolute? None of them seemed to apply at present as she sat cross-legged drinking black tea from a cup and saucer that had once belonged to Kay's great grandparents and discussing whether 'scone' should be pronounced with a long or short 'o'. Kay was not one hundred percent sure that they had taken to her but the 'interview' went well enough if perhaps the rapport they had struck up immediately with Em seemed to be missing. Still, it had taken a while to kindle the fire that now burnt in his heart for Pia. There would be time for them to warm to her. Yes, he was sure they would take to her in the end.

*

It was a gruelling journey to SW17. They had opted to follow their satnav on what purported to be a longer but quicker route along the M25 only to find that there were roadworks and the traffic was nose to tail most of the way. It was four o'clock by the time they arrived at Sandra's house.

Pia's mother was far from the person that Kay had expected. Somewhat overweight, she looked all of her fifty nine years but was trying desperately to stave off the ravages of time with excessive make-up, a probably all-over tan – doubtless fake, an anklet, arms and legs sporting a variety of tattoos and masses of costume jewellery. The contrast to her more natural daughter was quite dramatic. He was determined however, not to judge this particular book based on its rather flashy cover and greeted her in a cheery fashion as they were introduced.

'Nice to meet you Kay, I've heard so much about you,' said Sandra. So far, so good.

They entered what turned out to be a deceptively large Victorian house. Kay followed mother and daughter down a bright, corniced passageway ending up in the kitchen which proved to be chock full of gadgets; there was not one up to the minute kitchen appliance which Sandra did not possess. Instead of just tea or coffee which would have been the drinks menu in Kay's kitchen, he was presented with a dazzling choice of what appeared to be hundreds of variations on the same theme plus several varieties of hot chocolate. He opted for a skinny latte and was ushered into the front room which was dominated by an enormous wall mounted TV. A minute later he was offered a choice of biscuits from a large red tin and opted for a Chocolate Hobnob.

Sandra may have been trying unsuccessfully to turn back the clock but her hospitality could not be faulted. She was as conventional as her daughter was not. Much of her life seemed to revolve around watching soaps and any number of reality TV shows. He knew that Pia found this lack of a meaningful focus in her life very frustrating but try as she might, she had been unable to persuade her mother to join a club, any club where she could exercise either her body or her brain. As it stood however there can have been few moments in the day, thought Kay, when her backside was not in contact with the sofa positioned to face the TV.

When the three of them were together again, Sandra laughed and said, 'We're not much alike are we Kay?'. Kay could do nothing but reply in the affirmative.

'I put it down to her going to a posh school. Why His Nibs decided that was the right place for her I'll never know.'

It was Pia's turn to speak, 'Didn't do me much good did it Mum? All I got out of it was a semi-posh accent and a chip on my shoulder'.

Sandra addressed Kay, 'she was a nightmare as a kid'.

'I'm a nightmare now!' interjected Pia with a laugh.

'I've had worse dreams,' replied Kay almost seriously. Pia gave him a wry smile and pretended to stick her fingers down her throat.

Sandra had a shadow in the form of a Yorkshire terrier called Tyke who followed her round the house incessantly while continually emitting a high-pitched bark. At one point Kay bent down to pat the little dog and got his fingers nipped for his trouble.

'Oh, I should have warned you about Tyke,' said Pia, 'He doesn't really like men'.

'Thanks for telling me,' replied Kay shaking his bitten fingers.

Somewhere in the house, Pia's half-brother Christopher was lurking. She had described him as 'a bit of a recluse'. His sole interest in life seemed to be playing computer games, an entertainment that kept him occupied from morning to night. At one point, Kay thought he heard him coming down the stairs and prepared himself to be introduced to another member of the family. But nobody entered the room and shortly afterwards he heard footsteps heading back upstairs. Clearly the reclusive Christopher was to remain un-introduced to Kay.

'Would you like to stay for tea. You're quite welcome,' said Sandra after a while.

'No thank you Sandra,' replied Kay in a flash, 'we've got a long way to go and we'd better be heading back soon'.

*

'So what do you think of my Mum then?' asked Pia as they crossed Putney Bridge having decided to give the M25 a miss on the way home.

'She's erm… nice,' replied Kay as they continued in bumper to bumper traffic across the bridge.

'You don't like her much do you?' said Pia who was driving on the first stage home.

'I didn't say that,' said Kay, 'she's just not like you'.

'But is that a bad thing?'

'I'm not going to answer that one. I'll just end up painting myself into a corner. So let me ask you a question instead. Why didn't we meet your brother?'.

'Because it would upset him. He can't cope with meeting new people.'

'But you didn't say hello to him either'.

'Actually, I did. I stepped out to go to the toilet just before we left. I said hello to him then. He can't converse and gets uncomfortable if people are with him too long. Okay, perhaps I should have told you before. He has a form of autism. I think you might have guessed from what I was saying.'

The journey back to Ivywell was a slow one, taking three and a half hours. Travelling in the old Polo was not relaxing and Kay and Pia were shattered when they got back. Although they were not sure what degree of success attended their mission, they both had a sense that sufficient i's had been dotted and t's crossed to at least make the trip worthwhile.

Whilst he was not entirely convinced that his parents had taken to Pia as much as he would have liked, he had met Pia's mother and despite her conviction that he had taken a dislike to Sandra, this was not actually the case. She was just different to what he had been expecting and in a way reminded him of his paternal grandmother who he remembered as being addicted to Coronation Street.

Chapter Thirty Three

Kay could not help but keep an eye on Em's career and late that autumn he read that filming would shortly start on another movie starring Em and again directed by Monty McLay. In a departure from his previous work, this was to be a drama set in South Africa at the end of the apartheid era. To be titled *The Lioness* it would tell the story of a female community leader from Soweto and her struggle not only with the apartheid regime but with the sexism of the male establishment in her township.

Although he would never watch her films, Kay was once again in the position of frequently being reminded of Em's existence through an advert in which she featured. Five years before she had been paid a minimal rate to front the adverts for a down-market shampoo and a breakfast cereal. Today she was undoubtedly being paid a fortune for her part in an advert for a famous and very expensive perfume. Kay watched it and realised that from the pretty girl he had lived with three years ago she had now been transformed into an icon of feminine beauty. There could be few people in Britain who, even if they did not know the name, would not recognise the face.

Kay had never revealed the identity of his ex to Pia and this was the way he intended to keep things. But as it frequently does in the affairs of man, fate intervened with a resounding chuckle.

Pia's mother would sometimes give her the old magazines she had finished with and one evening Pia was browsing through a dog-eared edition of *Hello*. When she had got about half way through she exclaimed, 'Hey, there's a guy in here that looks just like you'. Pia looked at the picture, then at Kay, then at the picture again. Knowing what was about to happen, Kay got up from the armchair and ambled over to where she was sitting. There on page fifty one was a photograph obviously from an award ceremony showing Em and Kay arm in arm smiling for the cameras.

'Yes,' mumbled Kay. The moment he had been dreading had arrived.

'Yes. Is that it?' said Pia, 'the guy is the dead spit even down to that little mole on his cheek and you say 'yes?'

'Yes,' said Kay again.

Pia gave him a searching look.

Kay blew out his cheeks. He looked at the picture, 'That was at the 2012 BAFTAs. Em was specially invited'.

Pia sat there with her mouth wide open.

'So let me get this straight,' she said after a while, 'you went out with Emma Silvester?'

'Yes, although to be fair we stayed in more often than we went out. We lived together'.

'Why didn't you tell me?' responded Pia angrily.

'I did. You asked me to describe my ex. I did that. I said we split up largely due to her work taking her abroad and being

201

separated for long periods. Was anything I said there inaccurate?'

'Well no, but you didn't say it was Emma Silvester!'

'Look, I'd only just met you when we had that conversation. Would you have believed me if I'd said, 'oh, by the way my ex is a famous actress'. You'd have thought I was some kind of dreamer'.

'But she's stunning!'

'Yes, I only date beautiful women,' said Kay, hoping that this would defuse the situation.

Pia gave him a sideways glance, 'Don't try to butter me up Kay. We've been together for eighteen months now. I would have thought that in all that time you could have told me.'

'But when would be the *right* time? You're proving I was correct in not telling you. Whenever I did, it was bound to cause a scene. It's just that by chance you've found out for yourself. So, there it is, in a former life I lived with a beautiful and famous woman. Am I expected to suffer for that for the rest of my life? I'm happy with *you* now, can't you just accept that and give me a break?' But Pia was not to be placated. She stormed out of the cottage and Kay did not see her until the following morning. There would be no apology and for the first day or so, not much in the way of friendly conversation but bit by bit their usual relationship slowly resumed. However, Kay never risked mentioning anything relating to Em again.

*

Kay's immediate superior in the wildlife trust was a woman by the name of Joyce Colley. Now in her sixties she had had an eventful career in wildlife conservation. As a young woman she had been involved in projects in both South America and South East Asia, mostly involving aquatic and semi-aquatic mammals. These experiences had given her a deep love for the creatures that could be found in and around fresh water, a love that she brought to the animals that lived in the Wye and its tributaries. Joyce was due to retire at the end of the year and had already signalled that she would then be returning to her native Scotland.

Kay applied for the resulting vacancy and much to his surprise was duly promoted to a semi-management role which put his job on a par with Pia's. Within a couple of months, his photograph was on the trust's website above a caption which read; Mr. Kenneth Nettleton, Field Officer (West) and below a picture of Pia which read, Ms. Pia Cutbush, Field Officer (Central). In his former life, Kay would have thought the increase in salary that this gave him at best miserly, at worst an insult, but in his new world, the three thousand a year extra was actually quite useful.

The pollution levels in the river were worryingly high and Joyce had impressed upon Kay the necessity to regularly check the health of the animals, particularly the otters, to make sure they were not being affected too severely. As a result, otters received a disproportionate amount of Kay's, and therefore, Pia's, time. They would never complain though, as these were some of the most likeable creatures on their patch. To them, Kay added water voles, mainly because, as a result of predation by American mink, they were becoming increasingly rare but also perhaps because in his mind's eye he could see a fully clothed

Ratty rowing slowly down the river to see his friends Mole, Toad and Badger.

When he was working in London – it seemed an age ago now – work largely finished at the allotted time and the first thing that Kay wanted to do once he had left the office was to forget he had ever been there, but here his whole life was work and work was his life. All aspects of his existence merged into one but that was the beauty of it, he spent all his time doing things that had meaning to him and if he did not love the individual tasks - some could be both monotonous and physically exhausting – he could at least see that the end justified the means. The fact that Pia shared his passion was an added bonus. However strong his relationship with Em had been, their lives away from home were complete opposites. He was sure however that he had seen a little of his passion for nature rub off on her and he wondered where that would have taken them had it been destined to continue. But that was all in the past and their lives had taken radically different trajectories.

Chapter Thirty Four

July 2016

The trust was now being drawn more and more into the political arena as a result of the Brexit debate and although he hated doing it, on a number of occasions Kay was called upon to state the trust's position which had to be broad neutrality. He hated the division that the debate was propagating intensely. Like most of the people who worked at the trust, Kay believed that it was all very well to try and protect nature and the environment in one country but how much better was it to protect it in twenty eight countries? He did not however see proponents of splitting the United Kingdom away from Europe as enemies, but more as political adversaries, in his view misguided but they would doubtless say the same about him. Brexit was dividing the country pretty much down the middle and the two extremes were hogging the argument. Raj was far more isolationist than Kay and on the occasions they spoke on the phone, he always tried to avoid the subject in as much as it was possible to do. The last thing he wanted was to lose a friend over something as impersonal as an argument over politics.

When the result was announced, Kay had a feeling of being lost. He hoped that the country could make it work but had his doubts. Pia was more forthright. 'Fucking joke,' she said, 'why are we wasting our time over stuff like this when there are other far more important matters to be tackled. We'll spend the next ten years gazing at our navels and falling further and further behind'. But that was Pia, she knew her own mind, stated her opinions with conviction and really did not care whether others disagreed or not; that was *their* problem.

But then there was another side to Pia. There were times when she could almost be a stand-up comedian and this sense of humour could really tickle Kay. The very first time they had sexual intercourse and Kay was attempting in a less than adept fashion to undo the zip on her jeans she had stopped him for a second, looked him in the eye and said, 'I think you'll find that in this particular department, I don't live up to my surname'. Kay couldn't stop himself laughing, he hadn't thought of it that way before.

And she could do the absolutely unexpected. Just before twelve o'clock on one sweltering moonlit night that July, a night during which they had done nothing more exciting than watch TV clad in shorts and tee-shirts, Pia suddenly stood up and said, 'Come on, let's go!'. She threw Kay his trainer sandals, picked up a blanket, climbed into the Land Rover and waited for a bemused Kay to join her. When he had, she drove off into the night as fast as the elderly vehicle would allow. On arriving at what was clearly a place she knew intimately, she quickly undressed and gestured to him to do likewise. When they were both naked, Pia opened the door and stepped out with no hint of furtiveness or embarrassment. Kay looked around cautiously before following but Pia had already gone. She led him, sometimes walking, sometimes running, over a stile and into the middle of a meadow where silhouetted in the moonlight she led him in a slow, sultry dance before the two of them lay down on the blanket and made love. They remained there staring up at the stars with a tawny owl hooting in the background until the first hint of dawn began to break in the eastern sky.

On the way back to the Land Rover, they encountered a farm labourer making his way to work. They wished the startled man, 'good morning,' as if two people walking naked through the countryside at four o'clock in the morning was the most normal thing in the world. As soon as he had gone, they started to laugh and kept laughing all the way home.

*

There are many unexpected hazards that can afflict those who work in the countryside, everything from trip hazards resulting from old and forgotten fence lines through abandoned farm machinery to thoughtlessly erected electric fences. Furthermore, anybody who works in or around the Forest of Dean is very well aware of the threat posed by wild boar which since the late 1990s have reclaimed their ancient territories. People like Pia who came across them regularly understood their ways and were therefore in very little danger. The same applied to Kay who was now spending more and more time in the forest. It was thus typical that when he did receive an injury while on his patch, it was from a much more mundane and hence less expected source.

Not long after their early morning trip, Kay had been asked to give a talk to trust members concerning the recovery of raptors in the county following the DDT scandal of the 1960s. He had not received much notice and hence needed to put several hours a day into preparing his talk. Much of this he did at home but time was short and as a result he loaded a copy of his notes onto his mobile phone so that he could practice his delivery whilst walking in the countryside. On this particular day, Pia was visiting her mother in London but he was not entirely alone on his walk as Daniel had stayed with him and needed some exercise.

For at least two hundred years, the Hereford and its ancestors had been the beef cattle of choice over much of England. Generations of careful selection had bred a degree of docility into the creatures and as such, a field of cattle tended to go virtually unnoticed by those who lived or worked in the countryside. However, in an attempt to improve the growth rate of their cattle, from the 1960s onwards, many farmers looked to the near continent for inspiration. As a consequence, several varieties of European cattle were imported to Britain, not least of which were the French Charolais and over the years their numbers steadily increased. But such improvements have their price and where they were replaced, the natural stoicism of the Hereford gave way to the unpredictable and sometimes actually dangerous temperament of their French cousins.

So it was that on a pleasant Sunday afternoon, Kay and Daniel were strolling through an otherwise unremarkable field, Daniel pulling strongly on his lead and Kay heavily absorbed in learning his talk to what promised to be a very knowledgeable audience. The field contained a marked natural ridge and the footpath they were traversing ran obliquely for about two hundred metres to cut off a corner of the meadow with the ridge behind them.

Earlier that day, the farmer had turned out twenty five newly acquired Charolais heifers into this field and at the time Kay and Daniel came through the gate the cattle were still in the process of establishing their hierarchy. As they were hidden behind the ridge from where Kay and Daniel were walking, neither of them spotted the herd's presence until the sound of hooves could be heard very close by. Kay looked up to see one heifer, no more than ten metres away, kick out her hind legs and hurtle towards him. He immediately let go of Daniel's lead and the terrified dog made his escape, heading towards a small gap in the hedge just big enough for him to squeeze through.

Kay was not so fortunate. No sooner had he released the lead than the herd were upon him. The creatures were obviously most interested in Daniel but nevertheless seemed to be entirely unconcerned if Kay ended up as collateral damage. He was knocked to the ground and trampled by one heifer after another. To protect himself as best he could, he rolled up into a ball but in those few short seconds he knew he would be lucky to escape serious injury.

After the herd had passed to another part of the field, now determinedly ignoring him, Kay lay on the ground for maybe as much as five minutes, not unconscious but sufficiently injured to prevent anything more than the odd painful movement. Slowly, agonisingly he got to his feet. His left arm was extremely uncomfortable and he considered it most likely broken.

Breathing was torture and to make matters worse his mobile phone was another casualty of the stampede making it impossible for him to phone for help.

Painfully he staggered towards the far gate. Although only a hundred metres or so, this took him nearly ten minutes. Once through the gate, he again collapsed in the mud. A minute or two after this, and to his great relief he was re-joined by Daniel who remained with him, licking his face until no less than fifty minutes later they were finally discovered by a couple of hikers who phoned for an ambulance.

Chapter Thirty Five

July – October 2016

'You twat,' was Pia's greeting when she visited Kay in hospital that evening. He had suffered a fractured radius, five broken ribs, a punctured lung and extensive bruising. Kay gave her a forced smile through his oxygen mask but in the circumstances he was grateful for her less than sympathetic greeting. A simpering response to his predicament would not have been her style and would have worried him immensely. He was lying in the Accident & Emergency Department of the Gloucestershire Royal Hospital looking for all the world like an extra in _E.R._

The ambulance had actually been quite quick, taking no more than half an hour but the journey, with its bumps and lurches, was nothing less than excruciating. The hikers who found him had taken Daniel with them and following Kay's whispered instructions had asked one of his neighbours to look after him. Contacting Pia however, presented a different level of difficulty. His mobile phone had been ground into the mud and as she was simply in the list of contacts, he never looked at her number on his phone and had no idea what it actually was. So, in the end, the same neighbour had to intercept her when she returned home and give her the bad news. She was late but nonetheless turned round and headed back to Gloucester to arrive just after eleven o'clock.

The trouble was that Pia's psyche did not allow for much in the way of sympathy and instead she naturally attempted to use humour to raise his spirits. Under normal circumstances this would have been just what the doctor ordered but in his present condition, the last thing the doctor wanted was for him to alternately laugh and then try *not* to laugh when it hurt too much.

Kay was in hospital for five days and off work for six weeks. He had been lucky in that, give or take the odd bruise, his right arm had escaped largely unharmed. This meant that he was able to practice his drawing pretty much all the time. Copious sketches, some in colour, flowed from his pencils during those two months. Pia looked after him in her inimitable way, laughing at his misfortune and refusing to let him feel sorry for himself. If anything, they grew closer during this period, one in which she made the decision to vacate her flat in Cinderford. She had, in any case, been using it less and less before Kay's accident and was not using it at all whilst she was acting as his temporary carer. Jobs in the charitable sector are not the most lucrative and it would certainly save her a considerable amount of money.

Although he was a long way off being fit for work, after three weeks he felt fit enough to accompany Pia on her walks down to the river, keeping an eye, as they had been asked, on the otters and the other water creatures. They seldom saw any otters but that in itself was good news, they knew they were there and had they seen one in broad daylight, its lack of concern regarding humans might indicate that it was ailing in some way.

His enforced layoff gave Kay the opportunity to catch up with some old friends. Paul's wife Anna had given birth to another baby boy who they had called Oliver. Speaking to Jayne, Kay learnt that the DPP was attempting to extradite Tony Bailey from Thailand but it seemed that he had gone into hiding and it was possible that he had now left the country, presumably for another South East Asian state with little regard for who entered their land as long as they had plenty of money to pay bribes.

As Kay suspected might happen, Raj had become disillusioned with the bureaucracy at Legal & Provincial and had set up his own broking business with an ex-colleague. Although he only had Raj's word to go on, they seemed to be doing quite well and he had even managed to poach some of G & B's old clients who had not taken to the new regime when Levison Drake took over.

Rather disappointingly, his brother Jack had been released by Reading Football Club but in a silver lining to this particular cloud, he had been picked up by local club Wycombe Wanderers and despite dropping two divisions, was now not only closer to home but considerably closer to selection for the first team as well. The money was not great but Kay could never disguise his envy of his younger brother for getting much further in his footballing career than he could manage. He often wondered where his life would be now if he had never encountered Wayne Selby. Out of pure curiosity, he googled the name. It appeared that Selby had never made it as a full-time professional footballer but had had a reasonably successful career in non-league making a total of 421 appearances for Altrincham, Solihull Moors, Stafford Rangers and eventually Stalybridge Celtic. He had retired three seasons ago at the age of thirty six following a series of knee injuries. But did Kay envy him? You bet he did!

The one person he could not contact of course was Em. The internet gave him a lot of information about what she was doing but very little about what she was thinking. She had won a BAFTA for *Helen* and had clearly attended several award ceremonies with her husband. Furthermore, she was known to have a number of options regarding new films and was spending a significant proportion of her time in and around Hollywood. But annoyingly, there had been nothing recently along the lines of the interview she had given to Jodi shortly after *Herbert Square* when, under her friend's questioning, Em had been persuaded to tell perhaps a little more than she had intended.

Then, a couple of days before he was due to return to work, he absent-mindedly googled her name and up came an interview she had given to *Harper's Bazaar* the previous month. The interview started off dissecting her early life and her time at RADA, all of which was known to Kay. Then it took a sharp turn to reveal an aspect of Em that was new, or perhaps had just been lying dormant during their time together when most of her energies were going into kick-starting her career. The paragraph read:

'When I was a kid my Mum worked for the NHS. She wasn't a doctor or a nurse. Nothing like that, just one of hundreds of administrators at the local hospital. And she was paid a pittance, almost nothing. It makes my blood boil to think of it'. After a second's thought she added, 'We've got our society so wrong and I know you could point a finger at me and say, 'she's doing

*all right, why doesn't she give her money away?' Well, perhaps I
do, at least some of it, but when I look at all the footballers, the
bankers… yes, and film stars who earn a fortune and never…'
her voice tails off. 'What I think I'm saying is that people like me
who earn ridiculous amounts of money should be made to put
some of it back or society will just become more and more
unequal and people like my Mum will continue to suffer. It's no
use relying on our goodwill to make donations to charity. And if
that makes me sound political then so be it'.*
The piece continued. *'This summer, she received an MBE in the
Queen's birthday honours list…'.*

Kay stared at the screen, 'Christ on a bike,' he thought, 'where
did that social conscience come from?' It wasn't that he
disagreed with the sentiment, far from it, but it was just so
unexpected. The last time he had seen her, she had been
spending a large chunk of her income on clothes. Looking at her
photographs (in which he couldn't help noticing that she looked
fantastic…) it was obvious that some of her money continued to
be siphoned off to high-end fashion designers but he could
forgive her that as it probably represented a tiny fraction of what
she now earned.

And an MBE! That really was on the road to somewhere. She
was certainly not the youngest person to receive the honour but
even so, at her current age of what he quickly calculated to be
twenty nine, it was certainly a huge accolade. He wondered what
her husband with the mansion in Gerrards Cross thought of all
this.

After a minute or two he turned off the screen and headed up to the bedroom. He opened the wardrobe door and delved around at the bottom. Among old trainers and discarded tee-shirts he found a cardboard tube. Removing the end, he pulled out the contents which he laid out on the bed. 'Must be worth a bit,' he said to himself before dismissing such an ungallant thought. He looked at the picture, looked at it again and then slowly rolled it up, put it back in its tube and returned it to the ignoble resting place where it had remained for months undisturbed. It was obvious to him that Pia must never find this memento of his old life, so he piled up the junk at the bottom of his wardrobe to at least a foot high and shut the door.

Chapter Thirty Six

Autumn 2016 – Summer 2018

Pia visited the river to look for otters most days, usually in the evenings, and became very twitchy if for some reason she was unable to follow this ritual. Back in the summer she had discovered a holt about two hundred metres upstream from where the footpath leading from Ivywell emerged onto the river bank and had spent many hours watching and waiting for the creatures to appear. Sightings of the otters had become much more frequent. They were apparently getting used to her presence and would now come and go without taking the least notice of the strange human creature who seemed so interested in them.

Sometimes Kay came too but they seemed to sense his presence and there was no doubt that the most successful viewings happened when Pia was alone. There was no path at this point and to see them she had to duck under or climb over the branches of the osiers that fringed much of the river. This was not a problem for somebody as nimble as Pia and it only took a few minutes to reach her observation post where she would typically stay for an hour or so, simply watching and noting.

It was never quite clear how many otters used the holt but there was certainly a mother and two cubs. Now winter was nearly upon them, sightings became fewer and it appeared that the holt was less used than before but still she would visit as often as she could and was frequently rewarded with the sight of the mother and at least one of her cubs.

Pia was the sort of person who approached everything she did with a passion and it was obvious to Kay that their relationship was getting stronger and deeper as time passed by. They went to the pub after work less now, and spent much time in each other's company, making love frequently, perhaps less often than Kay had with Em but he told himself that they were older and perhaps time was giving them a foretaste of middle-age. As if to confirm this, the following summer they went on a walking holiday in Scotland, dropping in to see Kay's old boss, Joyce, on the way. They were able to give her the good news that the otters on the river seemed to be thriving. Joyce had transferred her love of nature to her new home in the Scottish Borders and spent almost as much time on voluntary projects as she ever did when in full time employment with the trust in England.

He had considered it before, but now Kay seemed to be constantly turning over in his mind whether to ask Pia to marry him. He knew her so well and yet was afraid that she would turn him down. He was not even sure why this mattered as their living arrangements meant that they were all but married anyway and yet he still feared the rejection. So, in the event he had not asked her to marry him that summer and they continued to live their lives much as before. Nonetheless, the idea remained in the back of Kay's mind. He would get round to it one day, perhaps next year, he thought.

*

Kay's job was continuing to develop. He spent more time on what could best be described as PR and despite his earlier misgivings, less on the nitty-gritty of reserve management. His day now often involved showing hordes of schoolchildren, mostly from Bristol or Gloucester, round one reserve or another, trying and sometimes succeeding in enthusing them about wildlife and the outdoors in general. It was a source of great disappointment to him how little many children knew about the countryside and, perhaps subconsciously, he saw it as his mission to persuade them to love nature as much as he did.

As before, he did the odd radio interview, was engaged as speaker for various interest groups and then one day was interviewed by John Craven on *Countryfile,* an event which he thought went particularly well, in fact, so well that the producer congratulated him on his performance. Kay loved his job but he was beginning to wonder whether there might be a place for him somewhere as a presenter of wildlife programmes. Pia had given him a sideways glance when he mentioned it.

'What do you want to do that for?' she said, 'I thought you liked your job'.

Kay thought he knew why she seemed opposed to the idea. His previous partner had spent her life in the public eye and this would perhaps be too close to the world of show business for

Pia's peace of mind. So for the time being he dropped the subject.

As summer approached, so did their fortieth birthdays. There was clearly a need for some sort of celebration, although as with anybody nearing such a milestone in their life, they both felt that there was now perhaps too much sand in the bottom half of their hour glasses for comfort. Nonetheless in the early summer, they put on quite a party. Raj and Kate came down from Manchester. It was the close season for football so Jack came too with his latest girlfriend Lily, who intellectually, if not physically, defied every possible convention of the budding footballer's wife. A year older than Jack, she was in fact, a philosophy student at Balliol College, Oxford. How on earth the two of them came to meet, Kay couldn't begin to imagine but fortunately they seemed to get along pretty well.

One of Pia's long-term friends who went by the name of Carol came along too. Their friendship went back to a time more than twenty five years ago when they had attended every protest march going. Whereas Pia had obviously mellowed somewhat over the years, Carol remained in her original unmodified form. Kay had met her before and this time was the epitome of 'once bitten, twice shy' and he tried his damndest to avoid her but to no avail. She button-holed him by the drinks table and gave him a full twenty minutes on how the Labour Party's chances in the general election, now just five days away, were being undermined by a cabal of capitalist lickspittles who had opposed Jeremy Corbyn at every turn. She reminded him of a kind of left-wing Mike Hancock spouting cliché after cliché about posh Tory twats and champagne socialists (despite Pia having told him that

Carol's father had worked for J.P. Morgan and her mother was a university lecturer). He eventually escaped, using the not unreasonable excuse that he really *did* have to use the toilet. He noticed over his shoulder that she immediately moved on to harangue his brother who truly was a political innocent. If it had not been for his Jewish ancestry, Kay thought, this would surely be enough to turn him into a Nazi overnight.

The party went on throughout the day and well into the long summer night. With the exception of Raj, Kate, Jack and Lily who were staying over in whatever little space they could find, most of the more distant guests had left by mid-evening. To Kay's very great relief this included Carol who had to be persuaded quite forcefully to board a cab in time to catch the last London-bound train from Lydney. The more she drank the more strident she became and by the time of her departure, Kay would quite happily have paid the entire cab fare back to London plus a generous tip for the driver who would no doubt have been suicidal by the time he got there.

When they were finally climbing into bed at two o'clock the following morning having drunk themselves sober, Kay, still wide awake leaned over towards Pia and whispered so that nobody else in the cottage could hear, 'why on Earth did you invite Carol?' It would surely have been evident to everyone, not least to Pia, that she had been driving the other guests to distraction. He had maybe expected an angry response but that was not what he got. Pia paused for several seconds before replying,

'I know she can be a nightmare but sometimes you have to show loyalty to people. There was a time in my life when I could

221

have gone one of two ways, the first towards drugs and dereliction, the other towards politics and protest. She helped show me that oblivion wasn't the answer and although the course I took wasn't easy - I was the original rebel without a cause - it did have the advantage of at least involving my continued existence and through a round about route has brought me to where I am. Without a Carol, I'm convinced there wouldn't be a me'.

She paused again.

'I guess I've moved on more than she has but I still have a warm place in my heart for her. So, you'll have to understand that there are times when Carol, difficult though she can be, needs to be considered. Does that answer your question?'.

*

Later that year there was another cause for celebration. On the Friday before the match, one of the Wycombe players let the manager know that the minor ankle injury he had picked up the previous Saturday was still causing him problems and as a result he was putting himself out of contention. The manager had taken Jack to one side and given him the welcome news that barring an unforeseen circumstance he was handing him his first league start. The word was soon out and by midday on Saturday, a large contingent of Jack's friends and family, including Kay and Pia, were making their way to Adams Park for the League Two contest between Wycombe Wanderers and Crawley Town.

It was a strange sort of debut. Jack was playing at right back and Wycombe won easily by the score of four goals to nil. He made a couple of important tackles and some good passes as well as the odd mistake but it was not the sort of game for a defender to take many of the plaudits, although the manager later told him that it had been a solid debut. Regardless of the result, his personal entourage of some thirty friends and relations were going to have a party.

Jack had only one more start and three more substitute appearances that season but it had given him a boost. The club finished third and were therefore promoted to Division One without the uncertainty and hassle of going through the playoffs. Despite being offered a new contract, Jack decided to move on and take up an offer from Forest Green Rovers. Money and the probability of getting more game time were the main reasons for this decision. A bonus was that he was only a few miles from Kay who could now be relied upon to watch him play much more frequently. Ordinarily that would very likely have been the case but this was to be a tumultuous year for Kay and by the end of it everything would have changed.

Chapter Thirty Seven

Summer – Autumn 2018

From late Spring the same female otter that they had watched the previous year was seen more and more frequently around the holt, a sure sign that she had cubs. Then on July 3rd Pia spotted not just the female but two small otters swimming uncertainly alongside her. She immediately named them Ada and Bob, although as yet, she had no idea of their true sex and after some thought named the mother Martha.

The intensity with which Pia visited the holt increased until she was spending almost all her spare time watching the comings and goings of the little family and recording their every movement on her phone. Bob was always the more adventurous of the two cubs and could frequently be seen attempting to eat everything from weed to floating twigs before deciding that these were not what otters ate and immediately trying something else equally unpalatable. Ada was more circumspect and tended to stay much closer to her mother, squeaking agitatedly when she felt unsure or threatened.

Day after day Pia would travel the short distance from the cottage to the riverbank and just sit there watching the otters. Sometimes Kay would walk down to join her but more often than not, he would simply not see her until nightfall whereupon she would regale him with stories of what the cubs had done that day - Bob caught a frog or Ada, her first fish. This observation of nature was part of Kay's job, so it was both useful and interesting but he couldn't help thinking that Pia was becoming slightly obsessive.

Then one day in early September Kay came home from giving a talk to the local W.I. only to find Pia sitting in the kitchen, her clothes caked in mud and her face streaked with tears. 'Bob's dead,' she said before he even had a chance to ask what it was that had clearly upset her so much.

'Why, what happened?' Kay blurted out, himself shocked by this awful news.

'I don't know,' replied Pia in a very flat tone, 'I just went down to the river as usual when I came home from work and before I'd walked more than a dozen steps along the bank, I saw his little body just lying there motionless. I picked him up and tried to revive him but he was completely stiff. I think he'd been dead for some time.'

There really was not much he could say to comfort her so he just sat there with his arms around her shoulders gently rocking her backward and forwards.

'We'll have to inform the Environment Agency,' he whispered after a period which could have been fifteen minutes.

'I know,' she replied. 'I've put his body in a plastic bag in the shed. I do hope he didn't suffer'.

'Did you see the other otters?'

'Yes, they were both there. Martha looked so lost. I really felt for her.'

Kay knew they were wild creatures who would naturally produce a surplus in order to ensure the survival of the species but he did not feel that mentioning that right now would be at all helpful, so he kept his own counsel.

At length Pia said, 'I know it's probably the worst time to mention this.'

He braced himself for more bad news.

'But I'm pregnant'.

Kay's mouth opened but for a good five seconds no words came out. They both wanted children although were not prepared to jump through the myriad hoops required to force nature's hand. If it happened, it did, if not there was plenty more life to be lived without them. In any case, Kay felt his sister Paula had done his parents proud by producing three children, albeit on the other side of the world. Doubtless Jack would ultimately sire a dynasty too. He felt no guilt on that score. But now, faced with the prospect of his becoming a father... well, he was awestruck!

When he had regained his wits he pulled Pia close to him and holding her tight said, 'Wow!'

'Aren't you going to say 'congratulations'?'

'Er... yes, of course. Congratulations. I'm just completely overwhelmed'.

'Don't worry. You'll make a brilliant father'.

'When did you find out?'

'This morning. Didn't you think I was a long time in the bathroom?'

'Well, no not really, it's not the sort of thing I think about.'

Pia was as fit, if not fitter than most women ten years her junior but a first child to any woman over forty would still worry a fair proportion of health professionals. These and many other thoughts went through Kay's head but ultimately he dismissed them. 'It'll be fine,' he thought.

*

The weather for the coming weekend was looking particularly bad. This was the fourth year that the combined meteorological offices of the United Kingdom and Ireland had resorted to the American habit of christening storms. Kay always felt that the names were a little too modern for his taste. Surely they would be more memorable if they were given daft old-fashioned names like Cyril or Cedric. Of course, it would be a pretty bad winter if they got as far as K for Kenneth.

This time however, Met Éirann had given the storm the rather unremarkable name of Callum. Kay did not know anybody called Callum. He did not know anybody called Cedric or Cyril either but he felt if he had the choice he would rather meet a Cedric or a Cyril than a Callum.

In any event, Storm Callum hit on the Friday with high winds and lashing rain and continued through a very wild night into Saturday. Pia had been unable to sleep, not so much because of the howling winds but more because she was fearful of what might become of Ada and her mother with the river threatening to burst its banks. Already the holt would be totally submerged and if they had survived thus far it would have been necessary for them to either keep swimming in the angry waters or seek sanctuary on the river bank wherever that now was.

Pia was suffering badly from morning sickness and her pregnancy made Kay feel very protective towards her which was a completely new experience for him. She was far from the ideal patient however. Twice he had intercepted her attempts to leave the cottage and head for the river. In whichever direction one was to turn after leaving the cottage, it would entail passing through a wood and one glance at the substantial branches now littering the garden, told Kay that it was a long way from safe.

Around one in the afternoon the power was cut off and unable to watch television or listen to the radio, they resorted to playing Scrabble. But Pia couldn't concentrate and they abandoned the game after a series of three letter words when she could clearly have produced something a lot more substantial.

She stood up and looked out of the window.

'There's nothing you can do,' said Kay for the umpteenth time.

'I've got to help,' she replied, 'Ada will drown. I know it doesn't look like I can do anything but there might be, you don't know.'

'It's too dangerous. Look at it!'. As they watched, a small rowan tree in next door's garden crashed to the ground in a flurry of leaves and displaced earth.

Pia sighed and sat down. The afternoon drew on into evening with no sign of the electricity being restored. Although the clocks had not yet gone back, night came in quickly and the rain continued relentlessly. They had candles but the only thing they could do by their feeble light was sit and talk and Pia was not in the mood for talking. They hung around, each in isolation, eventually retiring to bed at nine thirty.

Neither of them was able to sleep, Pia because of her concern for the otters, Kay because Pia could not sleep and was restlessly tossing and turning. All night the rain lashed down and the winds howled. His watch told the story of the hours, one o'clock, two, three, four… Eventually, and despite Pia's restlessness, Kay fell into a deep sleep.

It was nine o'clock when he awoke. Little had changed in the gloom outside. The wind was still dashing the raindrops against the window pane and rattling the old wooden frames, green leaves blew rapidly across the garden, jackdaws tested their mettle against each gust before turning and being swept along like small black Valkyries. But then, to his absolute horror Kay realised he was alone in the bed. Pia had gone!

He quickly got up and within a few seconds was dressed. Heading for the door he noticed, as he had feared, that her coat and boots were absent and there was only one direction in which she would have headed. He threw on his own boots and waxed jacket, opened the door and headed into what was a truly wild morning. He turned right outside the front door, facing straight into the wind with rain, small twigs and general detritus hitting him full in the face.

The path to the river was flooded to the depth of an inch or two for most of its surface and on several occasions he had to step over branches which were blocking his way. Before reaching the river plain, the path passed through a small wood, no more than two hundred metres across but enough to pose a considerable danger.

Once he had entered the wood he found that the footpath was obstructed in places by fallen trees and twice he was forced to take a diversion into the undergrowth to maintain his direction. When he reached the far side, he stopped. He could go no further. The river had broken its banks and was running a good fifty metres from its wonted course and now reached right up to the very edge of the wood. Over to his right he could see the osiers where the holt had been, standing in maybe a metre and a half of water. He called out, 'Pia! Pia!' but there was no response. He tried again, 'Pia!' but again there was no reply.

Kay spent a full hour alternately searching and calling but to no avail. After the hour was up, it gradually occurred to him that she was probably at home. Perhaps she had gone into town to get something? Yes, that would be it. He had been worrying for nothing. He hurriedly retraced his steps. On arriving back at the cottage he unlocked the door and in his cheeriest voice called out 'Pia!'

His voice echoed in the empty room. 'Pia!' he called again. The only response was from Henry who slowly sauntered out of the kitchen, stretched, yawned and came over to rub himself against Kay's legs. He called 'Pia!' for one final time. Again, no response. She was not there. He looked through the living room window. Both his Land Rover and her Polo were still parked outside.

He returned to the woods, all the time calling, 'Pia!'. He still had some charge in his phone so he called her number. After a pause the automatic messaging system cut in. 'Your call cannot be taken right now. Please leave your message after the tone…' Kay left a garbled message in what must have sounded a frantic voice and continued searching.

Again, he returned home. Still no sign of her. He decided to call 999.

The call handler was very kind but clearly she was desperately overworked. His call was passed on to Gloucestershire

Constabulary who answered almost immediately. He gave Pia's description and after answering a few questions about when she was last seen and what she was wearing, he was told that if they had any news they would get in touch.

After a restless half hour he called her mobile again but the result was the same.

It was now mid-afternoon and he had not seen Pia all day. Again, he went down to the river. Again, he was unable to find her. He returned home and paced up and down, overwhelmed with worry.

It was getting dark now and still there was no sign of her. The longer she was away, the more he told himself, that he had to face the possibility that he would never see her again. 'But people often go missing and they almost invariably turn up,' the police call handler had told him. 'Not in the middle of a storm they don't,' his sub-conscious had replied.

At eight thirty, the electricity was abruptly restored. It flickered for a while and then went off again. He used the remaining charge on his phone to call her number. Again it rang and again all he got was the automatic messaging system.

Once more, at nine twenty five the electricity spluttered into life. The voltage was clearly reduced however, as all it gave him was an anaemic yellowish light. He turned towards the kitchen and when he turned back, he gazed open-mouthed for there, seated in her favourite chair by the fireplace was Pia! How could he have been so stupid? She had been here all along! But that made no sense!

Pia turned to face him and smiled in the way that Pia always smiled which was as much a question as a smile, and when he thought about it later, as he often did, there was a hint of regret in it too. He stared open-mouthed, unable to believe his eyes, until he felt the need to blink but in the fraction of time it took him to open his eyes again, she had gone. He later learnt that this was called a 'crisis apparition', a far from unheard of phenomenon in individuals experiencing extreme concern about an individual close to them. Several people who lost loved ones on 9/11 reported experiencing such phenomena. Psychologists explain it as the mind's reaction to extreme stress but clearly psychics have a very different view. Kay was then and still would describe himself as an atheist but he had no satisfactory explanation for what he saw that day. The apparition of Pia seemed as real to him as she had been when he last saw her not twenty four hours before. In the succeeding years, he thought about it over and over again but an explanation was still as far away as ever. Nonetheless its effect on him was dramatic. He had not been frightened. In fact, in the few seconds that he was in the apparition's company he had experienced a warm, comforting feeling, the like of which he had not felt before or since. At times when the heartache seemed overwhelming, his memory of that feeling and of the smile, comforted and moved him forward to overcome his grief.

*

No more than a few seconds later there was a knock on the door. Still overwhelmed, he walked slowly over and opened it. There, standing in front of him, were two police officers, a man and a woman. The woman wore sergeant's stripes and was clearly the senior of the two.

'Mr. Nettleton,' she said in a soft voice.

'Yes,' Kay replied.

'I have some very bad news for you'.

PART 3

Chapter Thirty Eight

October – November 2018

The Piper at the Gates of Dawn may not be the most quoted chapter from *The Wind In The Willows* but it has a particular ethereal quality as the original members of Pink Floyd no doubt noted when they named their first album after it. Mole and Ratty have stayed up all night searching for a baby otter who has gone missing. In this quest they are helped by a compassionate demigod who leads them to where the missing cub is sleeping. For a few seconds, the two friends catch a glimpse of their celestial helper and the experience is overwhelming. In his kindness the demi-god decrees that to prevent their future lives being dominated by what they have experienced, they should forget, although a shadow of something great and wonderful remained.

As a child, Kay had read the book what, four, five times? It was not an exact analogy, it is true, but there were sufficient similarities for Kay to henceforward associate the events of that day with the amiable river-bankers who had illumined his childhood. In Kenneth Grahame's story, the benign presence rescues the baby otter and Mole and Rat return him to his tormented father. But for Kay there was to be no happy ending.

Pia's body was found on the far bank half a mile downstream from the holt. It was never firmly established quite what had happened but the presence of a large contusion on her temple seemed to point towards her having fallen and hit her head, maybe on a rock but that was pure speculation. Eventually, in a short hearing, the coroner would record a verdict of misadventure.

For a while Kay went around in a daze, unable to come to terms with the enormity of what had happened. Inevitably there was some degree of guilt but what had he to be guilty about? The decisions which led to her death had all been taken by Pia, headstrong to the last. His only crime was that he had overslept. Nonetheless, for many months thereafter those two little words, 'if only' were a constant presence in his mind.

There was a degree to which the extraordinary apparition Kay had witnessed salved his conscience as far as Pia was concerned but what of their unborn child? Thoughts of who he or she might have become and even what sex they were, ripped Kay apart. It was all so new, they had not even got round to discussing names.

Concerned about his reaction, friends and family headed for Ivywell to be with him. Being the nearest geographically, Jack, giving the lie to the popular image of professional footballers as selfish and uncaring individuals, all but moved in for the first few days after the tragedy. This entailed him withdrawing from the following Saturday's match 'due to a family bereavement' but clearly he felt that for once his family duties trumped his career. Ruth too came down for no better reason than to be with her son in what she saw as a time of great need.

In fact, what Kay really wanted was to be left alone with his thoughts for a while. He was not going to do anything stupid, he just wanted to come to grips with Pia's death and start the healing process but was unable to do so with all these people around. He knew they meant well but...

As it happened, the first time he was able to get away by himself he was witness to something which, although it did not remove his pain, certainly marked the point at which his recovery could begin. His first thought had been to get down to the river to where Pia was heading when, presumably, she met her death. Standing at the woodland edge and looking at the rapidly receding river, he saw a movement over to the right about a hundred metres away. He continued looking as a dark shape appeared, moving along the river's edge. A few seconds later the shape resolved itself into a familiar form - an adult otter, Martha he immediately thought. Trailing along behind was another, smaller shape. It was Ada! Had Pia managed to perform some magic to rescue the imperilled cub before her own death? It was comforting for Kay to hope so and for the first time in several days, he smiled and despite the tears coursing down his cheeks, did not stop smiling until he got back to the cottage.

*

Funerals can be many things. Kay remembered his grandfather's as a surprisingly joyous occasion in which the life of somebody whose time had come was celebrated with beer, cheese and pickle sandwiches and a lot of love. The tears that get shed on such occasions are often those of relief rather than unalloyed sadness. Inevitably Pia's funeral was different, the tears were of pure grief for somebody who should have had another forty or fifty years to their name. Sandra was inconsolable, her heavily made-up face streaked from eyes to chin and although Kay knew he should make common cause with her, he found it just too much. Other than a brief hug when she arrived, he deliberately tried to keep his distance.

Much to his surprise however, Pia's brother made an appearance; and after the service at the crematorium, he cautiously approached Kay and shook his hand. Kay appreciated this as he knew how hard Christopher would have found it to approach a stranger. Although he said little, his gesture opened the flood gates for Kay who was proving totally incapable of controlling his emotions.

On the periphery of the group was a tall, sandy-haired young man whom Kay did not recognise and, from his isolation, nobody else did either. After a while, and somewhat nervously, the young man approached Kay and introduced himself as Rupert. In the nicest way possible, Kay let it be known that he was not sure how Pia had known him. 'She didn't,' he responded. 'I always wanted to meet her but families being what they are, it was never er... encouraged...' he paused, barely able to control his emotions, 'You see, Pia was my half-sister... and it's just heart breaking that I will never meet her.' Rupert took a step backwards and blew his nose on a laundered white handkerchief. Kay could see that he was very upset and put his hand on Rupert's shoulder as a gesture of solidarity. Then it dawned on him, this was Sir Rupert Montgomery Standish, the 11th baronet.

Kay was surprised, firstly that he was there at all but secondly that he was far from the pompous upper-class stereotype that he had imagined. At Kay's request, he fumbled in his pocket and produced a card which revealed an address in Holland Park as well as the fact that not only was he a baronet but he was also a Ph. D. Kay felt a great deal of sympathy for Rupert never having known his own sister. He and Pia may have hated each other on sight but Rupert did not seem the kind of person to hate anybody and once Pia had got it out of her head that he was her brother and not merely the offspring of the father whom she despised, they might have got on just fine. It was one more item to add to the list of sombre situations currently stalled in Kay's head.

He received two dozen or so sympathy cards from friends or relatives who could not make it to the funeral. Most had come via his parents in Amersham but when he sat down to open the envelopes he immediately noticed one addressed to him in Ivywell, and in a handwriting that he knew well. Putting the others to one side he carefully opened the envelope. The message was brief but not unfriendly. It read;

'So, so sorry to hear about your loss. Thinking of you. All my love Em xxx'.

Kay was stunned. He had not spoken to her since the telephone conversation on that fateful late summer day more than six years ago. How did she know Pia was dead? And how did she know where he lived? It was completely mystifying. He made a mental note to get to the bottom of it. But mental notes are one thing, actually turning them into action, another entirely and it was nearly three more years before he got round to tackling the mystery.

Chapter Thirty Nine

December 2018 – January 2020

Kay declined to spend Christmas with his family that year despite their trying desperately to persuade him. His point of view was that if there was one time to think in silence of the recently departed then this was it. If he wanted company, he could always go to The Drovers. He knew that this would concern his mother in particular but he had not yet finished his mourning. The time would no doubt come when Pia would gently slip to the back of his mind leaving space for new situations and new relationships but that time was not now. In the end, he spent Christmas Day walking the countryside with Daniel who would always be a living reminder of Pia.

Working on the assumption that it would take his mind off his loss, he had returned to work as soon as he could but it was harder than he thought. The problem was that he had worked with Pia on so many projects and was used to bouncing ideas off her, tossing them about in order to come up with a conclusion. So many times the phrase 'I'll see what Pia thinks of this,' was the first thing that came into his head when faced with an issue. However, he persevered and gradually found different ways of working. It was not easy for his colleagues either, Kay thought.

After all, they had known Pia too and were now faced with the quandary of whether or not they should mention her name. In the end, Kay just had to say that Pia had been a part of all their lives and it really didn't help the efficiency of the unit if they pretended she had never existed.

Not for a moment did he question the conviction that he was doing an important job. Somehow however, the spark had gone. On and off over the next few months, he turned over in his mind whether he should stay where he was and hope that things improved or whether he should move on and get another job in his chosen profession somewhere else in the country. There was also a little voice in his head suggesting that perhaps he should do something more radical.

It had always been on his agenda to visit his sister, Paula, in New Zealand but now he was thinking beyond just a visit and perhaps not confining his thinking to New Zealand, maybe Australia, Canada? He had done some preliminary investigation on the internet and discovered that senior conservation jobs open to foreign applicants and not just natives, sometimes came up. But if they didn't, he could always go there as a volunteer and see what happened once his name became known. There was plenty of time and from a personal perspective, whatever happened, he would be content to see out the summer in his present position and then make a decision at the end of the year.

*

Kay had started going to the after work de-briefings again. They gave him something to do. His social life now revolved around visits to the pub, and long distance country runs to counteract the extra weight the beer was always threatening to add to his midriff became the new norm. Daniel would usually accompany him on these runs and if nothing else, he now had the fittest dog in Ivywell. He did not know whether his personality had changed since Pia's death, but he was finding it difficult to make friends and his evenings tended to revolve around various acquaintances he would meet in The Drovers or the other couple of pubs that he visited from time to time. In most cases he didn't even know the names of the people with whom he was conversing.

On one occasion he got talking to a complete stranger in The White Horse, another pub that he sometimes used. The conversation got around to women in the public eye and almost inevitably Em was mentioned. 'Lovely body,' remarked the stranger, 'what I couldn't do with that!' Kay gave a knowing smile which rather unnerved the stranger. He was not that bothered with people admiring Em's body, after all he no longer had access to it, but referring to her with the de-humanising pronoun, 'that' was a little beyond the pale. What was he going to do though, admit the relationship he had once had with her? This was a dilemma he had faced several times, not only on the occasion when Pia had discovered the photographs of them together. Only friends of long standing knew the story.

What had perhaps prompted the stranger's comment was Em's latest film. Breaking with her recent habit of acting largely in costume dramas, *The Blue Tarantula* was bang up to date. Once again set in the Caribbean (this time Jamaica), it concerned the turf wars between two international drug gangs. Controversially, it contained an extended scene in which Em, for the first time, appeared naked on screen. Even though the film had received 'mixed' (or even downright hostile) reviews, the presence of an unclothed Emma Silvester guaranteed considerable interest, if only amongst the dirty mac brigade.

Kay had, of course, heard about it but had thus far resisted the temptation to head to Gloucester Quays to watch the film. He reasoned with himself that he had not yet reached the stage in his life of going alone to the cinema just to see a naked woman, even if in this case she had once been his partner. Nonetheless, the first thing he did when he got home, following his encounter with the stranger was to reach into his wardrobe and pull out the rolled up drawing…

*

The more he thought about it, the more Kay was becoming wedded to the idea of spending some time, possibly the rest of his life, in either New Zealand or Australia. He had dropped Canada as there seemed little point in getting away from England's cold and miserable winters to Canada's even colder ones. He would let the cottage, at least at first and then if his sojourn became more permanent he would put it on the market. He felt bad about his parents – having two of their three children on the other side of the world would be hard for them but there was always Jack who would remain in England, at least for the foreseeable future.

Another big problem was the animals. Although he had never really wanted pets, they were now so much a part of his life that it would be a huge wrench to leave them behind. Logically too, it might be hard to find new homes for them and he certainly was not going to hand them over to an animal charity and an uncertain future. Their new homes would have to be hand-picked by him.

During that summer, Kay had a brief relationship with a woman called Claire. Five years younger than him, she was a doctor in General Practice, based in Monmouth. Although she was attractive and clearly very keen on Kay, it was just too soon for him. Pia still loomed large in his conscious hours and even larger in his unconscious ones. Had they met maybe a year later they would have had a chance but he had to accept that he was not quite ready and they parted amicably that October. Perhaps he could re-kindle his search for a partner when he got to the Antipodes?

All this time, he was researching positions in conservation anywhere in Australasia. It was not always clear from the adverts whether they were open to non-natives and so he frequently needed to ask the question by email. He soon learnt that when it was not mentioned, the answer was almost certainly 'no'. There were two that came up where the employer was prepared to do battle with the immigration services on his behalf but they were both in remote locations and Kay really did not want to go that far off-grid, so he reluctantly left them to the conservation hermits.

Eventually, early in the new year he received an offer of a position on the west coast of New Zealand's South Island. It was a lot further from the main centres of population than he would have liked but in all other respects it looked ideal. Like much of what had once been the British Empire, New Zealand was plagued by non-indigenous species introduced by the thoughtless British over a period of several hundred years and these were creating havoc amongst the local flora and fauna. Kay knew that when he arrived, tackling this problem would initially take up much of his time.

*

It seemed odd to him that he would be close, well okay, within a few hundred miles, of his sister. Throughout their formative years he and Paula had not always been on the same page, typified by her being a great fan of Oasis whilst he preferred Pulp. She was good at maths and hated history whereas Kay was the polar opposite. In sports they differed too, Paula played tennis - quite well as it happened, whilst Kay favoured football.

In the fullness of time, these differences would have resolved themselves as the inconsequential by-products of youth but when Kay was sixteen, Paula left for university in Leeds, only returning sporadically during the holidays. Before her course had finished, Kay had himself became a student and so their paths only ever crossed briefly. When her student days were over, Paula took a gap year to travel the world and whilst in Fiji met a young New Zealander called Mark. Apart from a few sporadic visits, she never returned. Hence their relationship was stuck in a time-warp of adverse circumstance.

And now, he was proposing to move in, metaphorically speaking, just down the road from her. It all seemed so strange.

Chapter Forty

January – March 19th 2020

Over the next few weeks Kay completed various online forms, applied for a temporary visa and investigated flights to Wellington. Much to his father's displeasure, his mother had agreed to take the cats whilst one of his work colleagues who had always liked Daniel was happy to take the dog. Kay would miss him and the memories that went with him. It was not his initial intention to stay for more than six months but if everything worked out, he would come back to England in the Autumn to sort things out and then return to New Zealand for the rest of his life.

Eventually he booked a flight with Virgin Atlantic for Saturday 29th March. This would give him three months to say farewell to as many friends as he could manage. Obviously Raj was on the list as were Paul and Jayne.

His mood at this time was a mixture of hope and melancholy. Hope that his expectations of New Zealand would be fulfilled, melancholy that there were parts of England that he may never see again, hence an additional reason for visiting Paul in Cornwall. As many people have noted before, there is something wild and primaeval about Cornwall, from the bleak granite moors to the crazy Cornish Alps and the gaunt remains of its tin and copper mining industries. And this might be the last time he would see any of them.

Paul's life had changed dramatically since he and Kay had worked together. About six months after Kay had transferred to Gloucestershire, Paul's wife, Anna had given birth to another baby. Four years later they had separated. She was still living in the family home, a pleasant Edwardian terraced house on the outskirts of Falmouth whilst he was living in a shabby two room apartment close to the centre of town, not unlike the one Kay had inhabited in Truro.

Paul had tearfully attended Pia's funeral because as Kay had surmised, he had always kept a place in his heart for her and that had been shattered when her body was dragged out of the Wye. But his living circumstances were less than ideal and as soon as Kay arrived on a rainy Friday evening, they repaired to a pub, in this case The Seven Stars, a rare example of what could be best described as an old fashioned boozer. Paul had put on a stone or so since Kay last saw him and was now looking every bit of his forty three years.

'The world's not been very kind to us lately,' Paul observed.

'Something has got to go right sooner or later,' Kay responded. It was not like him to wallow in self-pity but Paul's dishevelled appearance had made him feel lower than he had for a good while. But hey, he had the challenge of a lifetime coming up in a few weeks. He couldn't stay in the slough of despond with that on the horizon! Paul's expression however, indicated that he didn't expect things to get better any time this side of judgement day. Kay wracked his brains to come up with something cheerful to say but without success. Instead, he chanced his arm, 'So what really went wrong between you and Anna? You never gave me much of an answer when it all happened'.

'Put it down to irreconcilable differences,' Paul replied defensively, and then after a couple of seconds, 'no, that's not good enough is it? Partly it came down to my wish to move on, perhaps to do what you're doing and go Downunder. But she was born in Cornwall and just didn't want to leave. I love it here but there are other places in the world equally as nice. She just didn't see it that way.

And then… Well, you know how much time I would put into work. It was causing constant friction that I wasn't there to bath the kids and so on. It just all piled up and we decided, or rather she decided, that it wasn't working and I had to go.

Now I just see the kids at weekends and work my bollocks off during the week to pay for them. And would you believe she's got a new bloke who's bringing up my nippers? It bloody hurts'.

'So what's this guy like?'

'Ron? In some ways he's decent enough but thick as pig shit. I may not have been great at bathing the kids but there was a lot I wanted to instil in them as they grew up and with him involved I can't see them even being able to tie their own shoelaces by the time they're twenty one'.

'But you still see them at weekends'.

'Fat lot of good that is. I call round at ten o'clock on a Saturday morning, the door opens, my kids are pushed out, the door closes and I have to think what to do with them. My flat is a dump but there's nowhere else and what do you do in Cornwall during the winter? It takes me until Saturday afternoon to get them used to the fact that they won't see their Mum until Sunday evening and then we go and look at the docks or walk along a beach or something but it really isn't enough…'.

It upset Kay to see Paul at such a low ebb. He had been a massive help to Kay and a sympathetic ear when Em suddenly walked out of his life. Then, despite his own troubles had again offered sympathy in bucket loads when Pia died. But what could he do, other than reciprocate the compassion shown to him? He would keep in touch but even now he lived too far away to be of much use. In a few weeks he would be no use at all.

Kay had anticipated the possibility that the beer might flow when he met Paul and had made sure he stayed near enough to the centre of Falmouth to obviate the need to drive. After their sixth pint he walked with Paul back to his flat. Despite the dark, Kay could see the cracked pane and the paint peeling from around the window frame but could do no more than leave Paul there with the honest hope that his friend's life would soon improve. He headed back to his B & B with a heavy heart.

*

Kay was far from oblivious to what was going on in the world and the news from the East was troubling. There had been epidemics before, he remembered SARS, swine flu, bird flu… but it seemed that something had always kept the bugs in the Far East so they never got within three thousand miles of him. This one would be the same he said to himself.

But of course it wasn't. Just three weeks before he was due to leave, his sister sent him an e-mail;

Hi Kay,

Hope all is okay with you. Suffice it to say, this coronavirus thing is causing people here to panic. Our politicians are running around like headless chickens and people are saying we should just shut the doors and go into hibernation mode. I'm sorry to say this but it looks like your trip might be in trouble. Whatever happens you'll always be welcome here.

Look forward to seeing you. Soon.

Your big sis P xxx

This was no more than Kay had been expecting. The news had been full of coronavirus since not long after Christmas. Two days ago, the first death from the disease had been recorded in the United Kingdom. On 8th March Northern Italy, with a frightening number of cases, was put under lockdown and eleven days later, the one he had been fearing; New Zealand closed its borders to non-residents.

Chapter Forty One

March 2020 – March 2021

Lockdown came to Britain on March 23rd . Given that much of his work was outdoors, Kay continued working pretty much as if nothing had happened. The Trust accepted that he was not going to New Zealand any time soon and as they would not be able to get a replacement, just let him carry on as before. For the first few weekends he did pretty much what everybody else did, long country walks and bemoaning the situation to neighbours over the garden fence, at a judicious distance of course.

The three animals had been given a temporary reprieve from having to build new lives for themselves and for this, Kay was extremely thankful. Not only did it postpone farewells that he would have found heart-rending but their presence provided him with company in what could otherwise have been a very lonely existence. He did not know when it had started but he now found himself undertaking long, one-sided conversations with his pets. Sometimes Daniel would tilt his head to one side and at least look as if he was taking some notice of what was said to him but Pixie and Henry just carried on with their lives and ignored the idiot who was babbling away at them in some strange alien language.

Restrictions continued in varying forms throughout what was, from a meteorological point of view at least, quite a pleasant summer. Kay noticed that there were far more walkers to be seen throughout the countryside than ever before. There were complaints by farmers that people, unused to country ways were trampling crops, leaving gates open and generally making a nuisance of themselves. On the other hand, the lack of aircraft noise seemed to put life back to an earlier, simpler time when the song of the blackbird and the cawing of crows were the loudest sounds in his little patch of England.

And in a perverse way he was almost more sociable during lockdown than he had been at any time since Pia's funeral. The number of WhatsApp groups of which he was a member increased from half a dozen to twenty or so as small groups of old friends sprung out of the woodwork. There was one for school, university, ex-employees of Gresham & Bailey, Acton Athletic, his family and even one for the junior school he attended between the ages of seven and twelve, which included some individuals he had not seen for nigh on thirty years. He was constantly being sent internet memes that varied from simple jokes through political satire to some downright pornography sourced by an old school friend he had not heard from since he left for university.

On 13th November he received the troubling news that his parents had both caught covid. His father seemed to be holding his own but his mother's condition was cause for concern. The following day she was rushed to Stoke Mandeville Hospital and put on a ventilator. For the next two weeks she would remain in a critical condition, alternately rallying and relapsing before rallying again. And throughout this time there was not a blind thing he could do. The frustration was almost unbearable.

At the end of the month she showed three days of sustained improvement before going down again on the fourth. But the fifth, sixth and seventh days again showed steady progress and eventually on December 8th she was no longer considered to be in danger and was transferred from the Intensive Care Unit to a recovery ward.

The family all breathed a sigh of relief but it would be many months before she was back to anything like her old self. People were dying in their hundreds of thousands but this was his mother and the fact that she seemed to have survived a close encounter with the grim reaper had the effect of restoring his spirits to something like their normal level.

*

Kay had been very concerned about Paul and with all his problems, how he would cope during the pandemic, but it soon became clear that he was worrying unduly. Paul it seemed had discovered the joys of dating apps. This had led to a list, not exactly long but rather more than a short-list, of women to actually meet in person when the emergency was over. Kay breathed a metaphorical sigh of relief; his friend had seemed at such a low ebb the last time they met and this appeared to be one massive step in the right direction. In fact, when the pandemic was finally over, Kay almost wished Paul had discovered train spotting or flower arranging instead. Every few weeks he would call Kay and regale him with tales of his latest date, their seemingly athletic exploits between the sheets and pretty much anywhere else that took their fancy. It seemed to Kay that Paul was enjoying life again and good luck to him.

*

Kay had always been a glutton for wildlife documentaries so the restrictions imposed by the pandemic gave him ample opportunity to indulge his passion. One evening he switched on the television to watch a new documentary on BBC2 about the lives of Atlantic grey seals around the coast of the British Isles, when a familiar voice entered his living room unannounced. The pandemic had obviously caused as much disruption to the film industry as to any other, so it made sense that Em would temporarily direct her energies into areas where she could work from home, such as voiceovers.

His first thought was to reflect on whether the schooling he had given her into life outside the city had sparked an interest which she was now indulging or was it just a job of work for her? Certainly the programme was presented by Em with enthusiasm and, it appeared, considerable knowledge but she was an actor and so knew how to present a script.

His second thought however, was that he still had not established how she had obtained his address for the sympathy card which had arrived just before Pia's funeral. So after a few minutes thought, he decided he had to solve, or at least attempt to solve the mystery whilst it was still fresh in his mind.

It had to be someone who knew him and also knew Em well enough to have remained in contact with her after they had split up. He could not think of anybody. But as Sir Arthur Conan Doyle in the guise of Sherlock Holmes said in *'The Sign of the Four,'* *'When you have eliminated the impossible, whatever remains, however improbable, must be the truth'*.

So he phoned Raj.

It was not unusual for him to talk to Raj, in fact they would chat most weeks, usually reminiscing about their time at Gresham & Bailey but other times thoroughly prosaic conversations about sport, politics or pretty much anything else in the known universe. These were the sort of conversations that had made Alexander Graham Bell a very rich man.

After five minutes of general chat, Kay got to the point;

'There was something I wanted to ask you'.

'Okay, fire away,' replied Raj.

'Do you know how Em came to have my address in Ivywell?'

There was a long pause, 'I gave it to her,' said Raj hesitantly, 'I told her about Pia. She was very upset and wanted to let you know she was thinking of you. It wasn't the best time to ask whether I should let her know or not, so I just took an executive decision and told her'.

Kay thought for a moment, 'So how come you were in contact with her in the first place?'

'Through Facebook,' replied Raj.

Social media was anathema to Kay and from what he had seen, he was well out of it. Admass photographs depicting plates of unappetising food and cute kittens doing well, what cute kittens do, was certainly not enough to persuade him otherwise. And then there was the privacy aspect; he did not want the world and his wife to know his intimate details, even if he did not really have much to hide.

'Okay, let me explain,' continued Raj, 'One day about three years ago I got a friend request from a Mavis Tremslee.'

'Never heard of her.'

'Neither had I,' replied Raj, 'and to be honest I would have just ignored the request but the pen picture that came with it was clearly of a young woman and when I looked at it carefully I realised it was a picture of Em. That didn't prove anything though, people often use pictures of celebrities they admire. Then the penny dropped. I got a piece of paper and wrote it down. Mavis Tremslee is an anagram of Emma Silvester!'

'So why didn't she use her own name?'

'Because being in the public eye like she is, she'd be bugged to hell and back. Everybody would want a piece of her time. Now it might be possible to set up some sort of anonymous account but I wouldn't know how to do it and I'm guessing she doesn't either. It must have taken her some time to find me though. India is full of Raj Banerjees'.

'But why would she go to all that bother in the first place?'

There was again a long pause, 'Because it isn't me she wants to be in touch with. This is an account she keeps private, I'm her only friend, on this page anyway. She asked me not to say, so I'm breaking a confidence telling you this; all I get from her are messages and all those messages ever do is ask about you'.

Chapter Forty Two

March 2021 – Friday 29th April 2022

Snowdrops gave way to primroses and primroses to bluebells, covering the woodland floors with a sea of misty blue. The robin sang with renewed vigour and like miniature jet planes, swallows raced across the dappled sky searching for luckless insects. Although the papers still contained their fair share of bad news, one thing was clear, the pandemic was slowly coming under control.

On July 19th, all restrictions in England were finally lifted and in theory at least, everyone could get back to trying to live normal lives. This was not however, the case on the other side of the world where the governments were continuing to be spooked by even the odd case of the milder omicron variant. Kay of course kept a constant eye on developments but New Zealand's Ministry of Health never seemed to get out of first gear. He could understand their caution but it did him no good. That December, to make things worse, their Department of Conservation emailed him to say that in view of the pandemic, they were reviewing their requirements in regard to the job for which he had been selected. They would let him know the outcome in due course but nothing could be guaranteed. So the game of snakes and ladders that his life had become presented him with another anaconda.

As it happened, the next ladder was not too many squares away and it came from an entirely unexpected source. Throughout the pandemic, Kay had continued with his sporadic forays into the world of broadcasting, mostly on local radio but there had also been a brief interview on Jeremy Vine's programme on Radio 2. The following March, and entirely out of the blue, he received a phone call from the BBC in Bristol. He was not entirely sure how they had obtained his number but in this case he was not too bothered. The gist of the call was that they had been keeping tabs on his media appearances and wondered if he would like to drop in to discuss the possibility, no more than that, of becoming a (very) junior presenter on *Countryfile*.

The following Tuesday he got in his by now decrepit Land Rover and drove the twenty five miles to Clifton. If the person due to interview him had seen him in the car park he said to himself, he would have been offered the role on the spot - a thirty year old Landie was the archetypal *Countryfile* vehicle. The interview and screen test seemed to go well but he could now potentially be facing a conundrum. The job offer from New Zealand had certainly not been withdrawn completely; as he understood it they just needed to contemplate their navels for a while before deciding whether they wanted the hassle of shipping a foreigner from the other side of the world.

At best, the *Countryfile* role would be part time and if he decided to stay in England then he would have to find a way of combining it with his existing job. He suspected that the Trust would be amenable, especially as the executive to whom he gave his notice before covid struck had seemed genuinely upset to be losing him.

*

The WhatsApp group set up for ex-employees of Gresham & Bailey had been very active in recent days as they had, virtually unanimously, agreed that now, some ten years after they had gone their separate ways, it was the time for a re-union. It was to be a rather low-brow occasion, just a meet-up in a pub followed by a meal at an Italian restaurant in Great Titchfield Street not a stone's throw from the retail Armageddon that is Oxford Street.

The pub chosen for the occasion, The Cock, was the same one in which Kay and Paul had had a bit of a session after their chance meeting. It had been selected for the simple reason that it was one of the cheapest in what can be a very expensive area. At the very last moment, Raj texted in to say that he was suffering from some sort of bug that might have been a bad cold but was probably the current mild strain of covid. He did not want to be responsible for passing it on to anybody else and was therefore wishing everybody all the best but unfortunately they would have to proceed without him. Of course, Tony was not there either but nobody cared about that.

After a couple of drinks, the party left the pub and headed to the restaurant where Kay found himself sitting next to Jayne. She had married Dan just before the virus hit and was thus technically Mrs. Belcher but she informed anyone who would listen that there was no way she was going to be known by a name which gave the impression she had drunk too much lager and so Ms. Bentley she remained. She was also noticeably pregnant.

Most of the discussion around the table began with, 'Do you remember…' and from these three words flowed a whole torrent of reminiscences, two or three conversations at a time. The assembled company were reminded of the occasion when an unfortunate office junior had gone home with a two metre trail of paperclips attached to the hem of his coat and returned the following morning with only the first twenty centimetres remaining; the time when Mike left the office with a house brick in his briefcase and lugged it halfway across London to a client meeting near Heathrow Airport. There were memories of rubber bands and blotting paper in sandwiches, washing up liquid in tea, white emulsion in the milk bottle, shoe laces surreptitiously tied together under the unfortunate victim's desk and of course, there was Kay's little jape with the kipper, to which he had still to confess.

'You couldn't go anywhere near Tony's office for the stink!' said Nick.

'It had to be smelled to be believed,' chipped in Gill.

And then from Nick again, 'Did we ever find out who did it?'

'Personally I think it was Raj,' replied Kay keeping an absolutely straight face. 'You look at the circumstantial evidence. He was leaving about that time and hated Tony's guts. He's got to be prime suspect'.

Several people nodded their heads vigorously in agreement. Clearly his involvement with a member of the acting profession was paying dividends.

'Had to be him, he had all the motivation'.

'Hold on a second,' said Jayne turning to Kay, 'didn't you leave about the same time? And I can't remember you being so fond of Tony'.

Of course, Jayne had even more motivation than Kay, but he felt that bringing that subject up would be a little distasteful, so he kept his thoughts to himself and instead went into faux self-defence mode.

'How dare you insinuate such a thing! What evidence do you have?'

'Wasn't it you behind the raw egg outrage?' piped up Nick. This referred to the occasion when the hard-boiled egg in Nick's lunch box had been swapped for a raw one and the result had been a dry cleaning bill which Kay had eventually agreed to cover.

'But the yolk was on you!' replied Kay trying to deflect the accusation. There were groans from around the table. Doubtless this weak pun had been quoted *ad nauseum* at the time and a ten or twelve year hiatus had failed to give it even a modicum of respectability.

Sensing his opportunity, Nick picked up his dark blue napkin, put it carefully on his head and said in a stern voice;

'Kenneth Iolanthe Nettleton, I find you guilty as charged and the sentence of this court is that you be taken from here to a place of execution and there hanged by the neck until you are dead. And may God have mercy on your soul'.

'It weren't me your honour, it was Raj wot done it. I'm an innocent man!' countered Kay.

This was the kind of knockabout humour he had not encountered anywhere since leaving G & B and he realised how much he had been missing it. Although a sense of humour was not exactly lacking in either of the Trusts for whom he had worked, their employees tended to have a sense of mission, entirely absent in these disinterested wage slaves which meant that a higher proportion of wildlife conversations were serious in content, leaving less opportunity for play.

As the conversation died down a bit, Jayne leaned over towards Kay and said quietly, 'We've got him Kay'. It was immediately obvious that she was talking about Tony.

'Okay, tell me more,' Kay retorted.

'Well, you know I told you he was in Thailand'.

'Yes, but I thought you told me he had moved somewhere else'.

'He had. First of all we traced him to Vietnam, then Cambodia and finally Laos where he made a critical mistake'.

'Go on'.

'He got himself arrested for whatever the Laotian equivalent of gross indecency is'.

Kay's mind immediately dredged up the old joke of whether he had asked for another one hundred and forty three offences to be taken into account, it was that sort of night, but again he let it lie.

'So what he did next,' Jayne continued, 'was to contact the British consulate to enlist their help in getting him out of jail. They did a bit of research and found there was a warrant out for his arrest. And to cut a long story short, we're expecting him to arrive back in this country, hopefully in handcuffs, next week'.

'Brilliant!' said Kay but it immediately got him thinking. He had worked with Tony for six years and this seedy side to his character had remained unknown for nearly all of that time. And working with Tony had not been all bad. Although what was now coming out about him was not his only fault, he did have his good points. He could, for example, be funny. And generous. But all that would now be subsumed beneath those two words, 'sex offender'.

And in spite of what seemed to be his obvious guilt, Tony would eventually leave jail after, who knows, four, five, six years inside. Then he would have to make a new life for himself and what would that be Kay wondered. It certainly did not look promising even if he, Kay presumed, would still have enough money to make things a little easier than somebody from further down the social ladder who found themselves in a comparable position.

*

Kay had wisely taken the precaution of reserving a room at his parents' 'hotel' in Amersham. Despite the beer, the wine and not least, the company he found himself walking the mile or so to Marylebone Station in pensive mood. For some reason that he could not fathom, he felt just a tiny bit sorry for Tony.

The last copies of *'The Evening Standard'* were long gone from the stands at the station entrance but after walking to the far end of the concourse to use the toilet, he picked up a rather dog-eared copy on one of the red perforated iron seats provided for passengers' comfort. His train, the 23.57 was the last of the night and involved the long walk up to Platform 5.

When the station had been built for the Great Central Railway at the very end of the nineteenth century, it had allowed for only four platforms with sufficient space left for four more should traffic increase sufficiently to make them necessary. By the time of the notorious Beeching Report however, passenger usage had, if anything gone the other way and so the surplus land was sold off for development. Of course, what happened next was that demand for trains to Aylesbury, High Wycombe and points beyond did increase substantially making an additional two platforms not only desirable but absolutely imperative. Such unfortunately is the foresight of large corporations be they private or public.

To passengers' considerable inconvenience therefore, Platforms 5 and 6 were squeezed in, some one hundred yards from the concourse on the west side of Platform 4. To make matters worse, the clocks on the walkway to these far-flung outposts of the station sometimes told a slightly different, and often more optimistic, story to that on the concourse, lulling passengers into a false sense of security and for the unlucky, a justifiable sense of outrage.

Kay caught the train with barely thirty seconds to spare. Had he not done so, he would have been faced with a quick sprint to Baker Street in order to catch what regular users know as the 'Drunk's Special' and a slow and less than salubrious journey on the Metropolitan Line. Fortunately however, that had not been necessary.

Nonetheless, the pubs and bars of London, not to mention theatres, had provided sufficient late birds to make the train thoroughly overcrowded and he had to start the first stage of the journey to Harrow on the Hill, standing next to the doors on the last carriage of a four coach train. Leaning against the glass partition, he opened the paper, browsing from page to page, finding nothing to hold his attention for more than a minute or two. The crossword had already been started, incorrectly and in biro, so he retraced his steps towards the front of the paper. There on page two was something that made his heart race; *'Emma and Monty to Split'* the headline announced. Under a picture of Em, the article continued,

'BAFTA winning actress Emma Silvester and her film director husband Monty McLay are to split it was announced today. Emma, who starred in several films including Helen, The Lioness and more controversially The Blue Tarantula announced their separation on Twitter. The 34 year old actress said that they had not been getting on for some while and had been living apart since the beginning of the year. Monty McLay was unavailable for comment'.

Chapter Forty Three

Friday May 13th – Saturday May 14th 2022

A fortnight after his interview with the BBC, Kay received an email confirming that they would like him to present two short pieces in their summer schedule. What happened next would depend on him and the audience reaction to the appearances. Ordinarily he would have jumped at the opportunity but he still had not heard from The Department of Conservation in Wellington.

Finally on Friday May 13th, an email came through from New Zealand. Their review had been concluded and they were pleased to say that they wished to proceed with recruiting Kay to their team. Kay now had to think. It was not a simple heart versus head choice anymore and he really could not decide which option to go for. Although the deadline was not in fact Sunday evening, he felt that it made sense to have decided by then so a weekend of weighing up the pros and cons lay ahead. Saturday evening would not be a time for thought though, that was reserved for the F.A. Cup Final and he did not want to miss it.

At eight o'clock he received a phone call from Raj and Kay told him about his quandary. 'Tricky one that,' said Raj, 'but it's all good. Wouldn't decide too quickly though if I were you.'

Dropping the subject completely, Raj continued, 'Are you going to watch the Cup Final tomorrow?' This irked Kay somewhat as Raj seemed to be paying little attention to his future plans and Kay had a lot to tell him. For some reason Raj appeared to be keen to talk about the Cup Final, a subject about which, Kay knew, he had not the slightest interest.

'Yeah, all on my tod,' replied Kay, scarcely able to conceal his irritation.

'Who's going to win?' said Raj in what Kay couldn't help thinking was a disinterested tone.

This was getting silly, but Kay replied, 'No clue, probably nil-nil and then penalties.'

The conversation ended abruptly with Raj saying, 'okay, sorry mate, have to go now, got to put Sita to bed.'

All very strange. He had known Raj for fifteen years and spoke to him often but this conversation was unusually stilted and why had he wanted to talk about the Cup Final?

With so much going through his head, Kay slept very little that night, rising at four to make himself a sandwich and a cup of tea. After that he dozed for a while but still awoke at seven. He poured himself a bowl of muesli. Perhaps he would have preferred bacon and eggs but Pia had introduced him to a minimalist breakfast and he had no inclination to change the routine.

At ten o'clock he went outside to mow his little patch of lawn, weed the seedbeds and generally potter about beautifying the garden. The bird feeders were still hanging from the two trees that the garden possessed, a rowan and a hawthorn, but with the warmer weather the birds were visiting less often now. He had been pleased with the winter's haul – a blackcap had set up home in his garden and attempted, unsuccessfully it has to be said, to defend the feeders from all comers. As well as birds like the robin and blackbird, normally resident in gardens throughout the winter he had welcomed goldfinches, bullfinches, great spotted woodpeckers, his own little favourites the long-tailed tits and the occasional goldcrest. As ever, the sight of these active little creatures was sufficient to raise even the lowest of his moods.

It was a sunny morning which encouraged several species of butterfly to take to the air; first of all a female brimstone, followed by a red admiral and the pretty little holly blue. It had to happen; at just after eleven a small tortoiseshell put in an appearance and landed in the tree not one metre from his face. He put out a finger to try and encourage the creature to treat it as a perch and despite butterflies being very wary at this time of year, it stepped off the branch and onto Kay's finger for a few seconds before flying on to a neighbouring garden.

Of course he could not see a small tortoiseshell without being reminded of a time ten years ago when his life seemed to be heading in a completely different direction and from the evidence of the *Evening Standard* he had read two weeks ago, it seemed that Em's life too was at a crossroads. He wondered where this change would take her. She was guaranteed a place as one of the leading actors of her generation but what would it mean for her personally? He shrugged. It was all long ago now.

271

He bore her no animosity. In fact, he wished her well but still found it difficult to think about her without a hint of emotion.

He finished gardening at ten to twelve following a reminder from Daniel that he could do with a walk. The dog could be very persistent when he got it into his head that he needed some exercise. So they set off together for a walk across field and forest that would ultimately take them nearly three hours; three hours of Kay thinking he had made his decision only to reverse it in an instant and then go through the same process five minutes later. It was not going to be easy.

Chapter Forty Four

Although the game was interesting, it became obvious that goals were going to be hard to come by. The same had been true of the League Cup Final fought out that February between the same two teams. The result had been a stalemate, resulting in a nail-biting penalty shoot-out which Liverpool had won by the unusually high score of 11-10 after Chelsea's substitute goalkeeper, Kepa Arrizabalaga, who clearly was not expecting to be called into action this way, blazed the ball over the bar.

All the time Kay was thinking. Thinking. Thinking. One option meant a completely new life, new challenges, new people, new friends. The other was much of the same but with the added frisson of knowing that his words were being followed by millions. What to do?

Half time.

Kay got out of his chair and fetched another bottle of Butty Bach from the fridge. It was too cold but if he took his time, the latter part of the bottle would be just right. He would not get English (or even Welsh) ale in New Zealand it was true but this

273

was small beer… He grinned to himself over the small unintentional joke his brain had thrown up. They were sure to have something other than lager weren't they?

New Zealand!

His mind was made up. He would write to the BBC straight after the match, thank them for their interest but tell them his life was to take another course. Once he had done that he would write to the Department of Conservation and tell them that he had accepted their offer. He felt a sense of relief. In truth, he had been marking time since Pia's death and a new direction was what he needed. He felt a thrill in the pit of his stomach.

The second half kicked off but he was distracted. He was in a world of mountains, glaciers and bubbling mud. But he was also wondering what his parents' reaction would be. He felt for them but his mind was made up now, there could be no turning back.

The game rumbled on with no goals and no side getting the upper hand. His beer had nearly all gone and there was only one more in the fridge. Now or later? He opted for a Coke instead.

The second half had now finished. Both managers were standing in a huddle of their players expounding at length. With at least half a dozen languages spoken on each side, Kay wondered how much was getting through. Perhaps that was the reason for all the hand gestures?

The first half of extra time came and went without a goal. The teams swapped ends.

Five minutes into the second half his phone pinged. It was from Raj. There were no words, just a 'thumbs up' emoji. This puzzled Kay. What did it mean? Why had he sent it then? Had Raj suddenly become a convert to the great god Football? But nothing had happened on the field to warrant such a gesture. Perhaps he was telepathic and had somehow received news of Kay's decision through the ether? Stranger thangs had happened. He thought for one moment of Pia's apparition.

The second half of extra time concluded. Still no goals. His phone pinged again, perhaps this would explain the curious message from Raj? But no, it was from his brother;

'Effing overpaid Premier League players can't put the effing ball in the effing net to save their effing lives!'

This was an oblique reference to the last but one game of the season when Jack had scored a rare goal. It was a beauty too, 25 yards, like an arrow straight into the top right hand corner of the net and for the time being at least he was milking it for all it was worth.

Kay replaced his phone on the floor next to his armchair. It was all down to the penalty shoot-out now. Chelsea took the first.

Alonso (Chelsea)	scored	1-0
Milner (Liverpool)	scored	1-1
Azpilicueta (Chelsea)	missed	1-1
Thiago (Liverpool)	scored	1-2

James (Chelsea)	scored	2-2
Firmino (Liverpool)	scored	2-3
Barkley (Chelsea)	scored	3-3
Alexander-Arnold (Liverpool)	scored	3-4
Jorghino (Chelsea)	scored	4-4
Mané (Liverpool).	saved	4-4
Ziyech (Chelsea).	scored	5-4
Jota (Liverpool)	scored	5-5
Mount (Chelsea)	saved	5-5
Tsimikas (Liverpool)	scored	6-5

So it was a weary Liverpool who were going to be handed the trophy this year. He had no stomach for watching the post-match nonsense and had frankly had enough of football for one day. There was so much more to think about now he had made his decision.

After a few minutes, he took his laptop out of the drawer where it was kept and started writing an email to Tristram Walker his contact at the BBC.

'Dear Tristram,' it began.

'I know that this is going to come as a shock to you and it almost comes as one to me too, but after much soul searching, I have decided to turn down the opportunity to present two trial items for Countryfile. The fact is, I have accepted a job offer from New Zealand and will be leaving for Wellington within the month. I am so sorry if this upsets your plans but it was not a decision taken without a great deal of...'

Just then Daniel began to bark in a curious subdued fashion breaking his master's concentration.

'What is it old boy,' Kay said looking up from his laptop. The dog continued to bark quietly, as if to himself and headed for the door wagging his tail.

Kay rose from his seat to see what it was that was troubling him. He walked up to the animal and patted him on the head. As he did so there was a gentle knock on the door.

Kay was mystified. He seldom had callers and especially not in the evening. Cautiously he raised his hand to open the door. There was another tap. Louder this time.

After a further second or two he released the latch and there bending down to stroke a prone Pixie, was a young woman, slim and obviously not very tall; long, black, meticulously combed hair hanging so that her face was entirely hidden. Behind her he noticed a very new looking black Range Rover.

Now he understood.

She raised herself and turned round to look at him. In the pale evening light he could see that she was rather incongruously wearing sunglasses and obviously not to keep out the sun... After a second or two, Em raised her right hand and tipped her sunglasses so that she was peering at him over the top of the frame.

'Scuse me zir,' she said in a broad West Country accent, 'have you got a pownd for a cupper tea?'

Kay said nothing but just stared at her, his face expressionless.

Her clothes were simple; blue jeans, a tee shirt, well-worn trainers, all very similar to those she had been wearing when he first noticed the pretty girl on a train thirteen years ago.

But there was something else. She had drawn her hair back, enough for him to see that she was wearing colourful earrings and on each one the representation of a small bird. Slowly, slowly his face began to crack into a grin, then a half smile followed by a gentle laugh.

A second later, he felt her pick up his hand and press it to her lips. Then he could feel her laughing too, the enticing, liquid laugh that he had once known so well. She pulled him towards her and whispered softly in his ear, 'A friend tells me you have an interest in beavers.'

Kay roared with laughter.

She was already close to him but he pulled her even closer, kissed her on the top of her head and bending down, lifted her, Emma Silvester MBE, BAFTA winning actress, star of *Helen* and *The Lioness* bodily off the ground.

He turned, carried her inside the little cottage and still laughing, closed the door behind them.

ACKNOWLEDGEMENTS

I would like to place on record my thanks to Lorraine Boyd for her assistance in pointing out any errors in my original manuscript and for making numerous suggestions as to how it could be improved. Sincere thanks are also due to her partner, Ian Jarvis who designed what I think is an eye-catching and thoroughly appropriate cover for the book. Finally, I could not have got to the stage of publication without the help of my wife Chris whose understanding of and patience with technology is several thousand leagues above my own. For this, I believe she deserves a medal.

Printed in Great Britain
by Amazon